I0633143

WHITE ZION
And Other Stories

Gila Green

Červená Barva Press
Somerville, Massachusetts

Copyright © 2019 by Gila Green

All rights reserved. No part of this book may be reproduced in any manner without written consent except for the quotation of short passages used inside of an article, criticism, or review.

This is a work of fiction. Names, characters, places and incidents are a product of the author's imagination. Locales and public names are sometimes used for atmospheric purposes. Any resemblance to actual people, living or dead, or to businesses, companies, events, institutions, and locales is completely coincidental.

Červená Barva Press
P.O. Box 440357
W. Somerville, MA 02144-3222

www.cervenabarvapress.com

Bookstore: www.thelostbookshelf.com

Cover photo: Gila Green

Cover Design: William J. Kelle

ISBN: 978-1-950063-12-3

Library of Congress Control Number: 2019937331

ACKNOWLEDGMENTS

I wish to thank Shaindy Rudoff for starting a creative writing program at Bar Ilan University. May her memory live on through the door she opened for many writers. Thank you to authors Steve Stern and Mark Mirsky for believing in me before I believed in myself. Thank you to authors Allen Hoffman and Michael Kramer for your support. Thank you to Anna Levine, my writing partner and fellow ex-pat. Thank you to my friend Yvette Engelberg for helping with the cover photo. Thank you to Michael Keith for selecting *White Zion* and, of course, my gratitude to Gloria Mindock for publishing it with so much warmth and enthusiasm and a good eye toward everything. I wish to thank my sister Penny and my brother Steve for their constant encouragement. Thank you to my husband and to my children, who are simultaneously the beginning and the end of every path I take—always.

Thank you to the following magazines, anthologies, and presses for publishing *White Zion* stories.

The Wisdom We Already Know, *Akashic Books*, Mondays are Murder Series, June 2016.

Spider Places, *The South Circular*, Ireland, 9th Issue, March 20, 2014.

The Dalhousie Review, Halifax, N.S., Canada, 2006.

Nomi's Tomb, *Bridges: A Jewish Feminist Journal*, Ann Arbor, Michigan, Autumn 2006 (under a different title).

The End of Jewish Jerusalem, *Kunapipi: a Journal of Post Colonial and Commonwealth Literature*, Wollongong NSW, Australia. Vol XXIX, No 1, 2007.

Brass Knuckles, *Fiction Magazine*, New York, NY, Autumn 2007.

The Wedding Day, *Quality Women's Fiction*, Wisconsin, January 2008.

Roller Coaster, *Jewish Fiction*, December 2012 and *Sasson Magazine*, December 2018.

Reverse, *Many Mountains Moving*, March 2011

Different Rank, *Arc Journal* (title: Still Life with Father), Winter 2014, Israel.

White Zion, *The Saranac Review*, Plattsburgh, New York, Summer 2007.

Modesty, *The Boston Literary Magazine*, Spring 2008 & The *Mom Egg Anthology*, May 2008.

I Put Him on the Bottle, *Jane Doe Buys a Challah and Other Stories: An Anthology of Israeli-English Literature.* Ang-Lit Press, Tel Aviv, December 2006 & *Nothing But Red Anthology* New York, September 2008.

Arab-Israeli Assumptions is a version excerpted from my own novel *Passport Control*, S&H Publishing, 2018.

TABLE OF CONTENTS

Part One: Childhood & Adolescence

Part Two: Marriage & Motherhood

For the grandparents I was privileged to know, I am indebted. And for the grandparents I never met.

WHITE ZION
And Other Stories

Part One: Childhood & Adolescence

Spider Places

The apartment had only two rooms and a kitchen that felt crowded unless you were in there alone. As soon as you walked in you immediately bumped into something: an end table loaded with empty jars, a smoke-blue vase with lifeless, plastic flowers. The hallway was so narrow that the picture frames would shift on the wall as your shoulder rubbed against them, leaving streaks of dust on your clothing. There was a small rectangular-shaped veranda, but it made my Bubby nervous if anyone used it; even if the door to the veranda was open, she was on edge. Bubby was really my aunt, but she was so much older than my mother, a late life baby, that she thought of herself as our grandmother, and we thought of her that way too.

Whenever anyone came in, Bubby would be sitting there waiting on the green couch. It was striped varying shades of green, from very pale like wild dry grass to very dark, almost black. It had room for only two people, and if I ever slept over, it pulled out into a bed. Her large frame spilled over onto the second cushion, and I always hesitated a little before sitting. Scratching her psoriasis, she covered the couch and the floor around her feet with white flakes of skin like ashes. I had to brush off my jeans and my top before I got into the elevator when I left, but it was stickier than normal house dust, more like cobwebs.

Bubby wore enormous primary-colored dresses or equally large, vibrant tops with matching elastic waistband skirts. The tops often had V-necks and I would stare at the gold Stars of David or strings of colored costume jewelry in the wrinkled hollow above her bosom. It was difficult for her to do up her shoes because of her weight, so her red, or blue, or green shoe straps often dangled open around her thick ankles until someone, usually my Zaide, bent to do them up for her. She always carried a cotton handkerchief to mop up the sweat around her forehead and above her upper lip.

3

"You two aren't like the other two," she said to me often enough for me to know that she really believed it. She said it to me plainly, not maliciously, as though reading an inscription on my forehead. For her it seemed a fact of life; finger and toe nails grew long and needed to be cut or they broke off, hair dulled and grayed and my brother and I had foreign blood flowing around in our bodies, into our hearts and brains.

"You're half wild Indian," she'd always add. "Half wild Indian."

I could hear the chanting. "Ah yay, ah yay, ah yay." In my mind my younger brother and I patted our hands repeatedly over our opened mouths, hopping down on one foot and then the other in furry moccasins. There were long white feathers sticking up out of our tan, leather headbands. I could hear the steady rhythm of drums covered with the dried skins of dead animals in the background. Who was playing them? My father? We were protesting the government for burial and hunting rites. That's what Indians did in Ottawa as far as I knew; they sat unmoving like totem poles in front of the Parliament buildings waiting to dance and contort their half-bare bodies around the dry-looking men in stiff suits, who came and went out of the grand doors, and shielded themselves with their briefcases.

"I don't know what got into your mother, marrying an Arab after her awful divorce."

"He's Yemenite. A Jew from Israel."

"He sounds like an Arab. You look like him. Dark."

She'd place her chubby, itchy hand on my knee, and kiss me. Then she'd rub the redness on the tops of her hands until they were even redder, and I'd watch as more white flakes fell into the crack between the cushions of the couch.

"Well, I love you, dear. I love all of my grandchildren."

I don't correct Bubby. I don't point out I'm really her niece.

"I don't know where your mother gets it from. Not from me. She's like Ida. Not me."

Ida was my Bubby's older sister and practically a code word in her home. Anything associated with her was something she disapproved of, something one should keep at a distance like disease. She slipped phantomlike in and out of Bubby's conversations. No one except my aunt and uncle had ever seen her or heard her voice. There wasn't even an old picture of her among the crowds of framed photographs on my Bubby's walls.

"Oh, Ida disappeared in New York."
"Ida never married. No children."
"Never liked that I was the favorite, that Ida."
"Oh, she must be long gone."

But no one seemed to know if she was gone or not or if she did go when or how. It was as though most of her had burnt up in the chimney of my Bubby's memory banks. There were only some fragile charred bits remaining; she liked to shop, she liked to get her hair done. To questions like "why did she leave, how did she support herself, why did she never contact you," there were never any answers.

I sometimes sat with my Bubby on the couch waiting for a thin spinster with wild straw-colored hair to enter, perhaps through an open window or the veranda. She would be drained from decades of sifting through bargain bins in a larger-than-life city teeming with stores. She would be either drooling or licking the spit that had leaked out and down the side of her mouth. Loaded down with plastic shopping bags, she would have red circles around her wrists where the plastic handles had dug into her skin and mixed with sweat. My Bubby would look straight into her estranged sister's blazing eyes and wonder if she'd come for money. It was known that dollar bills and coins slipped out of Ida's hungry thin fingers like ice cubes in just-served soup. My Bubby detested wasters.

"I know you smoke, dear. That's okay. I won't tell your mother. Come on, share with your Bubby."

She reached out her reddened hand and I paused, reluctant. "It's okay. Got a match?" she asked me encouragingly.

Finally, I reached into the back pocket of my jeans and took out a pack of Player's Light. My hand shook a little as I offered one to her. She never inhaled. Still, guilt stung me. What if I killed her?

"I would have bummed one in the elevator anyway, dear," she said, smiling and putting her free, sweaty arm around my shoulders. She kissed me on the cheek.

"Want something to eat, dear? Here, I'll get up and make you something."

It was an effort for her to stand. She hauled her upper body into an upright position and heaved herself off of the couch. Her large frame touched both walls of the kitchen as she cracked eggs and looked for dishwashing soap.

The fridge door opened and closed, cupboards banged, cutlery was moved about and water ran in the sink. It took her about a quarter of an hour to emerge with a plate full of oily French toast dripping with Beehive Honey Corn Syrup.

I ate alone at the card table on one of the fold-up chairs my aunt had brought up from the games room downstairs after sandbag night. That was every Tuesday night.

I chewed without speaking. I knew she was sad inside for her only child, my cousin Allen. I knew he was dead only a few days, although I did not know exactly how many. I knew there was no grave. I kept chewing.

I tried to remember him, my Bubby's son, the skinny one, the baseball player, the geologist. He lived in the United States. He was married to a Gentile and he had two children. I didn't know their names or their genders. It just seemed to me like once in a while my mother would mention an

American cousin, but any questions I'd ever asked were greeted with a shrug.

"What happens to a spider when you step on it?" cousin Allen asked me one time during a break in the Passover meal. He wasn't married then. Before I could respond, he raised his foot up in the air and brought it down on the tiled floor. Whack!

"It's smushed."

"And where does it go?"

"It's dead."

"And where is it?"

"Nowhere. It's gone. Poof."

"That's what happens to all of us, Miriam. We aren't any different from spiders. Don't believe what they tell you in Hebrew school. One day all of us will end up like the spiders. Same place."

I remembered that now. I imagined myself a smashed-up spider on the bottom of a pair of cousin Allen's black, patent leather shoes, bits of me fallen away. I stopped eating.

"You know your cousin's gone dear, eh? You know that? Only thirty-five. It just spread right through him in only six months."

I nodded while I soaked the crusts of the white egg-bread into the syrup. I wanted milk to absorb the sugar in my mouth. I thought of my cousin's wide, laughing face, and his balding head.

"You were the cleverest baby," cousin Allen told me once. "Do you know what your first words were? 'That's ridiculous.' You were this tiny thing just over a year, running around saying, 'that's ridiculous,' to everything I told you."

As soon as my aunt and uncle heard about his sudden death, they boarded up their tiny apartment and got into their green Ford. It was a long, hot, ten-hour drive to some small, American town over the border, but my Zaide was terrified of flying. Scared stiff.

I don't know what those eight hours were like; if they could eat or drink on the way to saying goodbye to the son it took them more than a decade to conceive. I could see it different ways: my Bubby with tears dripping into her sticky, cheap, rosy lipstick, talking into the window pane about how it was a punishment from God. He had married out and God was putting his foot down all right. I could see it that way, or, possibly, she sat repeating his name over and over again mixed in with some traditional prayers my cousin would have mocked.

I am certain that my Zaide never said a word. He kept his eyes on the road, the road signs, the side and rearview mirrors, the red line gauging the gas burning up, his mind on crossing the border, getting over to the other side without any hassles about passports or ID. Maybe there was an occasional 'shush' or 'psht', but that's all there could have been.

At the end of the tenth hour they would have arrived at my cousin's large home. I had never seen it, but my aunt always said he lived in a mansion. He had married rich and done well on his own. The couple had prepared themselves mentally to say goodbye, to be greeted, guided. They longed to place a final kiss on their son's forehead or hand, to exchange whispers with some foreign nodding rabbi.

"I was ten months pregnant with Allen," my Bubby used to say proudly. "We thought he was never coming out I was so overdue, and he ended up over ten pounds. A big, baby boy, and look how tall he is today."

I remember my Bubby showing me newspaper clippings of Allen's baseball awards in the Jewish Athletes section of the *Jewish Bulletin*. He was always smiling into the camera, one hand confidently on his hip, the other clutching several gold trophies.

When my uncle had finished helping my aunt extricate herself from the passenger seat, they both noticed there wasn't another car in the long driveway. Their daughter-in-law responded to their knock, but over her shoulder there was only silence.

"We're here," Bubby announced in a trembling voice. "How are you? Can you take us to him or should we go ourselves?"

"No, I can't do that," my cousin's wife slurred, she was clutching an empty bottle in one hand.

"Can you just tell us where?"

"I mean, you're too late."

My aunt and uncle looked at one another and then back at their daughter-in-law's long face, her doll-like lips and reddened eyes.

"I had him cremated immediately. That's what he would have wanted. His ashes are—"

"Ah!" Bubby shrieked, her hands flying up to protect her ears. "His ashes? Cremated? Our son. Our boy. We've come to say goodbye. How could you not let us say goodbye? We came as quickly as we could. We want to say goodbye to Allen. Allen! Why didn't you wait?"

But my Zaide was already putting his white windbreaker on and tightening his black shoelaces. Then he puts his shaking hand on the doorknob.

"Izzy? Izzy do something. I want to see Allen at least. I'm his mother."

"Let's go, Bets, let's go," my Zaide said. His voice was just above a whisper. He had already opened the door wide.

"How dare she? How dare she? No asking, no telling, so fast, my God," my Bubby demanded.

"That's what he would have wanted," cousin Allen's wife repeated firmly, she steadied herself on the sideboard.

"What's wrong with you?" my Bubby asked. "We're his parents."

But my Zaide never heard these words. The engine was already running.

My Bubby staggered back to the Ford. Her tears mixed with the white flakes from her hands. The passenger door had been opened for her. When she sat down my uncle would get out of the driver's side, go around the car and close it. I never once saw my aunt straining to close the door herself.

"The *shiksa*! That lush! Ashes, my God, Izzy."

"Psht. Shush."

"But Allen, Allen. Where is he? No funeral, no stone, he's burnt up, all burnt—"

"Psht, psht, psht."

I imagine all of this while I continue to play with my corn syrup, drawing lines in it with the soggy crusts of bread. My aunt is as still as a totem pole. The cigarette has burned itself out in her hand. Neither of us look at the small pile of ashes on the floor. I watch a spider in the corner of the wall devour a mosquito, dead in her web, and inch my chair away.

Nomi's Tomb

I have always pictured her lying in the ditch, a throbbing pain in her broken leg. At first, she does not have time to digest the horror of what has happened. Is her leg broken in more than one place? I guess that it is not, that she has merely stumbled over some fallen branches or loose rocks in the ground, and tumbled into this would-be grave.

It is not long before she understands that she cannot allow her physical pain to immobilize her. Perhaps the sun is beginning to set already. She struggles like an untamed animal in a manmade trap. If she could only drag herself onto level ground, surely, she could retrace her steps, even if it means crawling on all fours at a loss to her dignity.

After a full hour of struggling to free herself, her strength comes only in stops and starts. With another hour's passing, her weariness is greater than any other force in her body and she succumbs to her exhaustion. Her final reality sets in: the pain, the fear, and eventually the wild hunger.

Forests are filled with animals. Maybe a lean fox appeared, momentarily stopping her heart while the last rays of daylight were vanishing beyond the thin treetops, or a screeching owl, whose pointy ears she could imagine, spooked her all night, keeping her alert and unable to hide in sleep. I don't want to push my imagination beyond that; an animal's teeth tearing into her arm while she is still conscious or biting an already shattered leg while she is not.

How many days does it take to die in a ditch in a forest? I have always been afraid to ask. By the time they found her body she had been missing for three months. Three months of rain falling on her dying, and then dead body, slowly disfiguring her features beyond recognition with the help of wind and the sun. Finally, a body becomes food for animals.

Sometimes I sift through old black and white family photographs looking for alternative images of my grandmother; something warmer to bury the image of the cold body in the ditch. In the first photo I ever found of her, she is dressed in mock royal garb: Miss Tel Aviv.

Four men are carrying her on a throne and she could be Batya or another Pharaoh's daughter out to tour her subjects. There were no talent shows or swimsuit competitions in the first half of the twentieth century. She is covered from head to toe in a dark, long skirt and a short jacket that triple buckles over her breast. A scarf peppered with tiny silver bells is wrapped around her wavy hair that is long enough to sit on and black as tragic loss.

There are several other photographs of my grandmother with her lips parted, but never really smiling. Here she is with a younger cousin, there with her parents. By the time color photographs were invented she had lost most of hers. In black and white she has skin that looks smooth as freshly peeled apples.

You feel as though you can look right into her eyes, they are so lucid in one photograph after another. Her hair is either swept over one shoulder or tossed loosely over both. She is dressed modestly, what people today would consider extremely modestly, but never without decorative collars and buttons on her tops and sashes around her small waist.

I turn a page and the black-haired beauty is gone. The photographs become colorful and she appears a timeworn figure, whose dull, shapeless wardrobe covers everything but her wrinkled face. She still looks at the camera, but her eyes are not readable anymore, only smudged.

My mother always recounts my grandmother's funeral in the same horrific terms she uses to describe her death, as though it were an extension of those months in the ditch.

"In Israel they wrap the naked corpse in a shroud and I could see it partially hanging out, you know, the feet, and half the legs. My God, you can imagine, after it had rotted all that time, exposed to the elements. I can still see it, even now. I will always see it. Your father didn't even show up. His own mother. He felt so guilty; he couldn't bear it. My God. In those days, the way they did things."

Then her mouth would close like an automatic door, her eyes would shift to neutral and she'd look away. Soon she'd be busy trying to make a dent in the permanent mountain of dishes resting in the sink or clearing off those awful orange place mats from that ridiculously impractical glass table. You always have to clean glass tables. Just place a cup of water on them and you have to clean them again. She seemed forever in the kitchen with her miniature bottle of fake clear-blue Windex, polishing away round semi-circles of water.

"Stop for heaven's sake!" I'd want to scream what seemed like half a million times. Instead, I'd just stand there listening to the jarring sound of the paper towels being ripped off the super-sized roll and watch, and my toes would curl in my shoes as I steadied myself: rage control.

I never said a word to my mother unless I felt it necessary; not one critical look would pass over my features aimed in her direction. I did not know how to communicate with her. No matter how much I ate, she always seemed to take up all of the available space. We could be filling out registration forms at a school function or filling our car up with gasoline. No matter where we were, people of both genders and all ages gravitated toward her. Everyone seemed to want a piece of her and there just wasn't enough left over between her assembly line of friends and acquaintances, her three husbands and her eight children.

"You're the eighth!" was something I heard all of my life and suddenly I would find myself being looked at with an entirely new expression, like I had an extra feature, maybe a tail or an antenna. What are your parents trying to do? Start their own country? That's what I always felt they were thinking. I never corrected their assumptions. A full explanation about my siblings and which one shared a father with whom only caused more squawking and excitement and it was a verbal examination I resented. I wonder if my grandmother would have understood.

My grandmother was only sixty-two or sixty-three when she died. She had begun to wander home to her mother and unspecified number of sisters, all of whom were dead. She would board the congested, raucous bus from Jerusalem to Tel Aviv without telling a soul and then search the streets uselessly for the home in which she was raised. The only home one would imagine that she had experienced love and security, warmth, and caring. She must have dropped in and out of sleep at nightfall in playgrounds or bus stops, eating only sporadically from food she might have stuffed into her pockets or handbag or maybe even garbage cans. By the time a few days or a week had passed, some policeman would find her and bring her back to her three remaining sons in Jerusalem.

My father had left for Canada while she was still young and capable. He never saw her as his younger brothers had: clumsy and forgetful, an inconvenient burden on the shoulders of three men and their wives trying to raise young families. I have often thought it might have ended differently for her if my father had had a sister instead of three brothers. Women forgive parents for things that men never will.

What could I have learned from my grandmother? I know that she spoke Hebrew, Arabic, and Yiddish. I can hear myself counting to ten slowly in English, waiting for that elderly nod of affection, that slow smile of understanding. Then I lean forward and it is my turn to wrap my tongue around the foreign Arabic words in exchange for the final sweet we both knew was always mine.

"They had a miserable marriage those two," my mother always said. My father rarely referred to either parent, and when he did, details were sparse. "Your grandmother was separated from her family in Tel Aviv from day one. In those days there was an unreliable bus between the two cities and it was an uncomfortable, bumpy and smoky ride, so she rarely saw her family. It wasn't like today with the modern roads and air conditioning. As she approached sixty, the longing for her family would overcome her and of course, she'd forget they were dead. Then it would take your uncles a week to find her and bring her back. They figured she'd be safer in a nursing home, but she didn't want to go. She was relatively young and strong and she liked taking care of her own little house, her own things."

All I remember of my grandmother's house was her doll collection. I was five and overweight from too much Kentucky Fried chicken, dripping with the honey they'd give you in those bite-sized plastic containers, and I was as shy as any fat kid in a foreign country.

I remember a room with low ceilings and walls that felt too close together, and an ancient woman, who covered her hair and neck with a night-blue scarf, opening the thin wooden doors to a closet which was filled with the dolls she had spent many years collecting. I cannot remember any specific doll; I see only a jumble of bright eyes and plastic grins of different shapes and sizes in neat, dusted rows.

My grandmother was pointing at the dolls and smiling down at me, and I hope I smiled back, but honest to God I don't remember. I know that chances are I stood like my own young daughter often does when confronted with a stranger: shrugging a shoulder up to one ear, mouth ajar, eyes unnaturally wide. I hope not. I hope I made her smile that one and only time.

"So, they finally called your father and asked him," my mother continued.

When the table gleamed to her satisfaction, she would finish the story over the same cup of instant coffee and buttered roll she'd been eating for breakfast ever since I'd known her.

She never finished a cup of coffee, but always stopped drinking it halfway. Cold chipped mugs of Taster's Choice or Nescafé decorated our house like rubber plants or picture frames in other people's homes. The non-dairy creamer she preferred to milk would rise to the top as the temperature of the liquid dropped, forming an imperfect white ring around the inside of the mug. I remember it like someone else might recall dried toothpaste on hand towels.

"He was the eldest and that means something to them. Ridiculous—he hadn't lived there for fifteen years, but he agreed. I don't know what choice he really had from so far away. They were tired of calling the police out to look for her, but she knew what they were up to. The Alzheimer's, you know, had just started and in those days what did they know about it? Senile, she's going senile was all they said and it was a burden on them. But she missed her mother and her sisters. After the divorce she'd let herself go, aged before her time. At forty, she looked sixty, and at sixty? And believe me she was beautiful once—Miss Tel Aviv at sixteen if you can believe that. It wasn't acceptable in those days to get divorced and he got this new big house and new wife and six new kids, while she became a cleaner and baked Yemenite pitas for passers-by in the front yard with the chickens all around. God."

I remember the day my parents came to tell me she was dead. They entered my bedroom together and asked me if I wanted to sit down. But my father was gone before anyone had a chance to say a word.

"Your grandmother's dead," my mother blurted, like the cleaning fluid spraying out of her miniature Windex bottle. "She's been missing for months and I didn't want to tell you. I mean, you only met her once. Well, she's dead. Died in a ditch. I have to go to Israel tonight for the funeral. Your father won't go. He'll stay with you. His own mother, the coward. Men are all cowards, Miriam, you might as well know that now. They stick out their chests, but they are all cowards. Your father is no different from the others. When David was four with encephalitis meningitis and I went to see him beside that child with the huge head, oh, he looked like a monster, and there I was already pregnant with our third one, your brother Joseph, and people clucking like ailing hens and they were quick to say to me, *Well, you've got Sara and another on the way, it's not like you don't have other children.* Do you think he came once to see him? One time to that horrible hospital room?

I don't know how I could have dealt with it if it wasn't for your Bubby coming and screaming and shouting and making them put him in a different room. 'How do you expect her to visit him here with these other children around terrifying her? Do you want her to lose the baby?' You got to have some inner strength too, you know. I have to pack now," she interrupted herself.

She looked for rather too long at her cheap, gunmetal watch. I knew she was stalling while she considered whether or not to say something nice and comforting. She chose to half exhale, half sigh and left the room.

I threw myself on my second-hand bed, my head buried in my hands. I had never known a dead person before and all of those smiling plastic dolls were spinning like summer tires stuck in the ice, round and round in my head going nowhere at all.

My grandmother had run away from the nursing home her sons had forced her into and no one had witnessed her escape. It must have been in the late 1970s. It seemed not one policeman in all of Israel could find her.

Three months later some backpackers were walking in the forest, just three kilometers away, and they came upon the ditch. The ditch that was her grave, her tomb. She wasn't sealed in, of course, but she couldn't escape. She lay in her wall-less tomb and no one knows how long she was conscious; what she thought or felt. But what does anyone feel when they know they are in a deathtrap? Did she assume someone would come by any minute to save her and adopt the repose of merely waiting for salvation? Or did she retreat mentally into her dead mother's arms, spared by the Alzheimer's, the root of her death sentence? Did she pray to the God she couldn't see, the one whose rules she had followed since birth or curse the sons who had snatched away the freedom she lost her life trying to retrieve?

I have neither erased her death from my mind nor found a place to put it where it will lie still. "Hush," I sometimes find myself whispering at night to a wakeful ghost. "Hush, there's nothing for it now."

My father's mother, whom I hardly knew, born in Tel Aviv when it was still Ottoman Palestine, died slowly, in pain and alone, starved, dehydrated and abandoned in Jerusalem in a ditch—the way forgotten women do.

Borderline Boarders

When I was thirteen my parents lost their restaurant business and we were forced to move into a smaller house. We called them condominiums. This means all of the houses were attached in identical brown rows and someone else cut our grass in the summer and shoveled our snow in the winter. We were no longer on an avenue or a crescent, but a road, 13A Bell. This was the beginning of the boarders.

"It's cash money in the bank," my father explained and that was enough for him.

"Your brother doesn't sleep in his room, anyway. We might as well rent it out." He added this superfluously. Who was going to challenge him?

My brother, Our-Stanley, only fourteen months my junior, had a bedroom in the basement because there were only two bedrooms upstairs and I had already claimed the bedroom next to my parents' room. Aside from Our-Stanley's basement-bedroom there was a small washroom with a toilet and sink only. Boarders would have to shower upstairs. There was also a laundry room that was part weight room, storage space, and spare bedroom.

It was true that Our-Stanley only ever slept on the brown couch in front of the television set. How I disliked that couch with its dark brown, velvety texture, and little gold-colored beads, which created a bumpy borderline around each individual floral pattern.

My father clumsily spread faded, white sheets over it, which did nothing to improve its appearance. The sheets hung loosely over the back of the couch, and they were not changed often enough for my taste. He believed the sheets made the couch cooler to sit on in the summer months, although they remained there year-round. No one in my house could fold or even seemed to believe in the act, so this untidy couch-bed dominated the living room. Our-Stanley was well on the road to becoming a bona fide insomniac and, when he did sleep, it was during the daytime, so his bedroom downstairs was arguably available.

Our first boarder was French Canadian from Trois-Rivières, a typically Catholic Quebecois town. He came with his textbooks and his guitar case, a ready smile and a relaxed manner. Luc must have been twenty, but to me he was an adult, and I was enormously flattered every time he gave me the slightest bit of attention. He introduced me to instrumental music, and he often shared his tapes with me in the evenings when he was home. He spoke to me softly, like I was an equal.

He would gently point out the different instruments we were listening to on each cassette. His collection was small, but he assured me that he had recorded each tape we listened to from his much larger album collection at home.

Each cassette was labeled in large slanted printing. A-cappella: he taught me that word. In the spring he packed up his guitar and his books and he left as he came, with a smile and a handshake.

"I'll mail you a new tape from Trois-Rivières," he promised, to a girl who was used to disbelieving all of adults' promises. He proved himself to be a man of his word, and I did receive a cassette of the songs he knew were my favorites, and I was grateful. But this initially stable ground became shakier after Luc.

The second candidate to respond to my father's newspaper advertisements was a Jewish girl from Winnipeg; a cold, flat, and isolated city in western Canada. Helena had one sole obsession: marriage. I had never and have never since met anyone with the same starvation to be coupled as Helena, although I am sure now that she is not unique. To look at her was neither to look away nor to look twice. She had average length, average color brown hair and eyes, large, black glasses, and a wide mouth. She was not fat, but completely round (breasts, stomach, thighs, and bottom).

When my parents were out of the house, which was often, she would march up and down my beige carpeted upstairs hallway to the wedding music she had chosen. I can still see her, a smile like a flare in the middle of her face that lit up her eyes. She always tilted her chin forward at these moments, displaying absolute confidence and composure: a bride.

Our-Stanley and I spent hours gawking at her as she lost herself in the reverie of her wedding day. She invited us to join her for these wedding parties, and she was disappointed when our attendance was low.

The fact that she had not even one phone call from a potential suitor did not touch her dreams. Up and down, back and forth she pranced, occasionally offering a slight wave or a secret smile to one of her imaginary wedding guests. Her mother? Her about-to-be mother-in-law? I never knew, but I was mesmerized by the intensity of her make-believe.

After close to an hour, Helena would tire and collapse on her bed, directly into her heap of bridal magazines. She had several subscriptions. I lived in a house where purchasing a magazine was considered an utter waste of money, so I was amazed by the audacity and magnitude of her magazine collection. Here was someone who not only spent money on magazines, but she had actually subscribed to several of them about the same topic.

Helena did not so much pore over these items as pour into them. She was all but sucked into their glossy pages. Each article revealed yet another insight into the wedding ritual: "White Hot Weddings" or "Writing your Wedding Vows the way Poets Do."

She inhaled all of this information, but it was all an aside from the icing on the cake: the wedding gown. She spent much time confiding in me what she was going to wear, which garments the bridesmaids would don; there were more decisions to make than drops in the ocean.

The wedding jitters brought out Helena's appetite. We always ended up downstairs in our kitchen, where my mother allowed each boarder separate shelves in the pantry and the refrigerator. The same meal was prepared every day:

three fried eggs upon which she poured an entire can of Campbell's Cream of Mushroom soup. Our-Stanley and I never ate with her, but we always kept her company for the three or four minutes it took her to down her giant omelet in runny white sauce.

Winter came and went and spring arrived. Soon the magazine clippings of veils and flowers began to disappear from the end tables in the living room, and Winnipeg called once again to Helena. There went the bride.

I doubt our third renter daydreamed about honeymoons in the Caribbean or cloth napkins with matching nail polish. His name was Rob and he was in the army. It is common in Canada for young people in the army to study during their military service. He was from Sarnia, a very small town near Toronto.

He looked the part to a T: lots of khaki clothing, black hair, crew-cut, wide and strong as a moving truck. He was not much of a talker and he was no music lover like Luc. No, I don't have those kinds of memories to tell you about Rob, for we never spoke, and our only communication was a rare, hurried, and uncomfortable meeting of the eyes.

The army did not keep Rob busy enough. I realized afterward that he must have spent a lot of time snooping around our house during the day. Both of my parents worked full-time, and it was a long school day for Our-Stanley and I that ended only after an hour and fifteen-minute bus ride home.

When whatever rental agreement Rob had signed with my father ended, he was gone, and we did not think much about it. After all, how often does a fourteen-year-old go to the bank?

When we were twelve and fourteen my parents took us down to the Canada Trust, where they had always held bank accounts, to open a savings account for each of us. I had a newspaper route, and Our-Stanley had birthday money and they decided it was time for us to have accounts in our own names. It was not difficult to discover these facts if you lived with us for a while and forging the signature of a thirteen-year-old is an easy task for most adults.

Several months after Rob left, Our-Stanley went down to our bank in the strip mall at the end of the road. In a few minutes he discovered that his bank balance, which had previously been around $14,000, was zero. He had passed his bar mitzvah already so, although he was young, he had acquired a relatively large amount of savings. Guests traditionally gave generous checks to mark this important occasion. After many arguments with the bank manager, we finally got the money returned to us from the bank, but my father had learned an important lesson.

"That's it!" he announced one night, while we were all sitting in front of the television. Most important family discussions took place during the commercial breaks.

"No more students. From now on, I will only accept people on welfare; a guaranteed government check at the beginning of every month, and not too smart."

His face turned back to the television and he resumed his previous pose. I met my mother's eyes and pleaded silently with her. She gave me that look, "What do you want me to do? Start a fight?" I looked away. I had been enjoying the few months of boarderless existence.

This was the beginning of a series of fourth, fifth, and sixth boarders. A blur of strangers, all of them male, began to enter our home at all hours of the day and night. They lived in the basement, no kitchen privileges, and my father had a makeshift shower put in beside the washing machine. They surfaced only in the dead of night to use the phone.

"Yeah, pizza. Combination."

I heard this often being muttered into the receiver, normally between two and four a.m. before I would hear the sound of footsteps retreating down the stairs. Lying in my bed, I would picture a shadowy male figure. He would be clad in thin brown or gray corduroys, wearing a tight blue or white T-shirt and worn-out white gym socks with a home-rolled cigarette tucked behind one ear. Sometimes it was obvious that two or three people were living down there.

"Dad," I dared to complain one day over my breakfast cereal. "I'm sure the boarder is letting in his friend through the basement window at night. He is sleeping down there for *free*." I emphasized this last word, hoping to provoke an angry response.

"What do I care?" was his curt reply. He waved his large hand in my face. My father was exhausted from working all night, flipping hamburgers in a fast food restaurant.

"I get the check. Cash money."

The basement was now a horrifyingly squalid place, where I would only descend when I was forced to get my laundry. Normally my parents brought up the washing, but once in a while, there was that shirt or pair of socks that I had to get.

I did this only in the daytime, and while holding my breath for as long as humanly possible. Even approaching the small bathroom was unthinkable. The stench reached up the stairs into the front hall closet, and the varying smells from the bedroom and laundry room were equally thick and revolting. I never invited a friend over from work or school. It was unimaginable.

There could be someone walking down the street with a key to my house, I would think over and over again on my short walk to school. By now junior high school was over, and I was no longer enduring long bus rides home.

The local high school was just across the street. Knowing that any depraved, drunken lunatic could be let into our house at night was scaring me, infusing me with a kind of subtle paranoia as I roamed the neighborhood. Even if I had nothing else to do, I avoided going home.

Then one day the money I had earned from my after-school job waiting on tables was gone. Someone had lifted up my mattress, where I had taken to putting it before I got to the bank and removed it. It was not a clever place to put cash, but this was my bedroom. I approached my father again.

"Fifty dollars? Big deal. I'll give it back to you," he replied and shrugged one strong shoulder.

I took the money. I bought a lock for my door. I lay in my bed at night wondering who had searched my bedroom. Was he sleeping downstairs right now? Was it the friend? A brother maybe? Was he coming back? I began to lock my door, even when I was home, which was less and less.

Then one day in the middle of the night it ended. It had been four years. I had spent the night at a high school dance. Really, I had spent three hours dressing and undressing, mocking myself the entire time, before I finally showed up in the foyer of my high school.

I proceeded to spend forty-five minutes staring at the webs of adolescent bodies sticking and unsticking themselves together on the enormous dance floor. For the second half of the evening, I slinked upstairs to the second floor where the non-dancers were grouped off smoking different brands of cigarettes in the maze of locker bay areas.

After watching the last dance, which was always a slow song played as slowly as possible with the lights dimmed as low as the teacher on duty would allow, I went outside. I hung around by myself for a few minutes; I was never in a rush to go home. Finally, there was nothing to do, but cross the street.

As I approached the first row of brown condominiums, flashing red lights caught my attention. It took me a few seconds to realize that an ambulance was parked in my parking lot, and a few seconds longer to see that its destination was my house.

My mother was watching television in her floral pajamas alone when I left. My father was at work, as usual, and Our-Stanley was driving around and around the high school dance in one of his second-hand sports cars. I knew that my mother would be in the same position when I came home: Glued to a drama series, eating one of her favorite night-time snacks, most probably refrigerated Del Monte canned peaches in heavy syrup and full fat cottage cheese.

I quickened my pace and opened my unlocked front door, holding my breath. Inside my living room I saw two medical attendants trying to communicate with our latest boarder. I can honestly say I had never even seen him.

Now I got my first and last long look at my father's definition of cash money in the bank. His dirty brown hair was spiked about ten inches off of his head. He was white, thin, and he looked about thirty, but he could just as easily have been twenty-two or thirty-eight.

He was unremarkable, except for the hairstyle and he wore typically faded jeans and a baby blue, checked shirt. His face was as stiff as a new pair of shoes, and he was banging his forehead repeatedly against our living room wall. It must have hurt, but he made no sound. I did not see him blink.

My mother appeared to be her usual passive self. I imagined that if she was at all distraught it was mostly over the interruption of her television show and the change in the temperature of her fruity dessert. If it is not cool right out of the fridge, it is not as refreshing. She had told me this many times.

After about six or seven minutes of quiet coaxing, the medics managed to convince our boarder to proceed out of our house, and into the ambulance. As he was helped across the living room, down the six steps into the front hallway, and outside into the ambulance, his head bobbed forcefully up and down, as though our living room wall was still in front of him, or perhaps as though he had never moved from the wall.

My mother and I said nothing until we could hear the sound of the ambulance speeding away, its jarring siren a stern warning in the night. For half a second, I wondered if any of the students still hanging out in front of my high school had seen it and if so, had any of them connected it with me. I turned to my mother, my face a heavy bold question mark.

"I was watching my program," she said quickly, grabbing for her peaches 'n cheese at the same time. "He came up the stairs. I don't remember his name. He wanted to use the phone. Said he wanted a pizza."

She paused there. I nodded, as though this happened in lots of homes.

"You know, I don't like it when they come up, and I am sitting here in my pajamas, but there is no phone downstairs."

I nodded again. Even a teen girl could fully understand why you wouldn't want a mental patient to come up from downstairs, like litter coming in from the seashore, and make a mess of things.

"Anyhow, that was it. He headed for the phone, but he stopped suddenly and he immediately began banging his head against the wall, just like you saw. Your father had mentioned that he was recently released from the R.O."

The R.O. is short for the R.O.M.I. or The Royal Ottawa Mental Institution.

"I called them right away. They said he must have forgotten to take his medication, and they'd be right over. And they were, like you saw." My mother paused again and sighed.

"So...that's it I guess."

Her undecipherable brown eyes rested on me for a minute, and then she turned her head toward the television set, and settled back into the couch. I watched her spoon her fruity dessert into her mouth, her cocoa brown lipstick leaking into the whiteness of the cottage cheese.

I don't know what I was waiting for. I knew that there would not even be a tiny bit of, "My, oh darling, can you imagine what might have happened if you had been home alone and...."

I left her there, absorbed by her television program, and went upstairs. I took out my bedroom key from my front pocket and unlocked my door. I don't know why I looked around the room, as I was the only one with a key. It was a habit I had taken up after I discovered the stolen money. I sat down on my bed. They did not let patients lock their doors at night in mental institutions. Tonight I would leave my door unlocked too.

The End of Jewish Jerusalem

I have no idea how my father met Eshkol, but there have never been more than a handful of Israelis living in Ottawa. Eshkol's television sales and repair shop had an oblong white sign hanging outside, the kind you see on cheap motels with large navy blue lettering: Open Seven Days a Week. My brother, Our-Stan, and I hung out there on Sundays and sometimes after school. This allowed my mother to shop uninhibited and my father felt toward days off like other people feel about running out of gas or milk.

"Life is *avodah*, work," he'd insist when my mother would ask him to take a break. "I don't know who told you Canadians life was about happiness."

I never knew my father was Yemenite until I was already in university. My mother had told me he was Israeli and he was not a talker. I knew he was as strong as the desert heat and just as relentless. The clang of barbells hitting a floor or clashing together still make me think of him; his powerful inhales and robust exhales that could tilt you off balance if you weren't careful and stood too close.

To watch my father doing his daily workouts was to fill your being with a potent mixture of admiration and fear. Admiration that the human body could be capable of such physical strength; there were dozens of framed photographs on the basement walls of my father on his back with his hairy, dark brown arms and legs in the air balancing all eight of us kids on his four limbs and smiling with ease into the camera.

Then there was the fear, the shattering sounds of impact: fist meeting plaster, plaster giving way to muscle. It's a good thing his own father apprenticed him to a carpenter, it made it a breeze for him to fix the holes his flying fists or his muscular heels put through the walls. It made it cheaper, too.

My eyes often lingered on the fathers of my friends in my Jewish Orthodox primary school. They wore neckties and suit pants and looked like they were on their way or had just come from temperature-controlled rooms.

My father wore the identical pair of plum-blue shorts all year round with wide strapped brown or black sandals and pink, green or yellow short-sleeved button downs that he only ever buttoned half way, revealing his massive, hairy chest.

I am convinced that he got those shorts looting makeshift Egyptian army bases when he was a paratrooper in the Sinai War. I even mentioned this to him once.

"Oh *vadai*, we take lots from them. Blankets, food, you know, cans? My mother blessed me she was so happy. In Jerusalem it was freezing."

"And your shorts?"

"What these? The blue?"

"Yes those."

"You going to help me match the socks or you going to talk *shtuyot*? Now you don't like my shorts?"

In the icy Ottawa winters when the radio was instructing the public to leave each tap running slightly so the water pipes wouldn't freeze, expand, and burst, my father added a winter coat to his wardrobe, one that reached the edges of his shorts.

His exposed thighs and calves were covered in black hair curling out of his dark brown skin. His thin neatly-trimmed, black moustache sat on his purple lips that hid gleaming white teeth. He had no idea that to the average pale, thin-boned Ottawan he looked like a dangerous foreign flasher. As a teenager from October through March I dreaded escorting him into the bank, which he often asked me to do as his spelling was not good enough to fill out withdrawal and deposit slips.

I held my breath as he pulled back the heavy glass doors; were people simply going to throw their money at us before they fled or push some red button that would signal the impending arrival of a police car?

"Abba, it's minus thirty outside. Your legs are naked and you're wearing a long coat. Please can you put on a pair of pants?"

"I put on boots, okay? This make you feel better?"

"No, Abba, a big coat, bare legs and boots? They will think you're a flasher or a thief or both. Can't you take mom to the bank?"

"What does it mean flasher? Your mother with me in a bank! She only spends money. If she knew what I save, she would buy more junk for the cupboards. When I was a kid, I do whatever my father told me and I don't tell him what to wear, so don't get too smart."

I pictured my father then as a twelve-year-old boy in Israel's first year of life: 1948. He was late for school again. He had spent too much time in the provisional control room on his roof, inhaling the sights and sounds of the emerging Israeli air force.

There were pilots practically within arm's reach speaking in low tones as they boiled water for their first cup of coffee. A few of them were sleeping in makeshift tents or single worn-out sleeping bags, but most had already scraped the last of the *dysa*, a hot breakfast cereal, out of their bowls and were preparing for another day of war.

"Assaf, get the leftovers while they are still hot. Assaf!" his mother called to him in Arabic. She does not speak *Temani* like his father, only Hebrew and Arabic.

Assaf scattered the rest of the yellow grains to the five rust-colored chickens they kept in their front yard and began to climb the wooden ladder the soldiers had attached to the back wall of their stone house: these were the stairs to the airport headquarters.

"Hello, boy," said the first soldier he saw as he stepped onto the black, freshly tarred roof. "It's Assaf, right?"

The boy smiled. He cannot understand the soldier's question. A Jewish soldier, who spoke Hebrew in a strange accent, told him there were men here from unimaginable places like Canada and Austria and many were not Jewish. They were all volunteers, eager to help the new Jewish state.

"This must be very exciting for you Assaf, eh? Imagine the roof of your house is full of soldiers, your field an airport, a boy's dream, eh?"

The twelve-year-old smile re-emerged, but his mouth did not move.

"Well, here's your breakfast. Take it while it's hot. You're lucky we always get more than enough. Beats your rations, eh? Maybe in the afternoon there will be some candy for you and your little brother."

I watch him pat Assaf's head and return to the heap of maps and papers that covered a turned-over crate that doubled as a table. The boy stole another minute to watch him as he picked up his walkie talkie and began to speak. Soon the pilot was deep in conversation with another soldier. They were marking up the maps in different colors: black lines that closed off parts, red lines even they couldn't cross, blue circles of open spaces.

Six soldiers had their heads stuck inside small airplane engines in the recently flattened large field behind Assaf's home. He could hear them tinkering with the metal parts, the occasional curse in Arabic, Hebrew or English erupted from their mouths as they struggled with something heavy or something that would not come loose.

Every few minutes their heads popped up like rabbits emerging from their hiding places, and they sipped steaming cups of muddy Turkish coffee and took long drags on their cigarettes as they paused.

There was the constant whine of airplanes overhead, the occasional sound of a shell bursting in the close-by center of Jerusalem. On the ground the chickens were fighting, squawking loudly for the last seeds on the hard soil in the front garden. Strange languages reached his ears and he watched the accompanying vivid hand gestures the men used in order to make themselves understood.

"Assaf! Your little brother is hungry."

His mother's voice penetrated his thoughts. He became conscious of the hot pot of dysa in his hands. He stirred the cereal with the wooden spoon his mother gave him before he climbed the ladder and turned in the direction of his kitchen at the same time.

"Ima, I'm coming."

In an instant he was inside his own kitchen and his mother was spooning out the dysa into small, white, hard bowls.

"So nice of the soldiers to give us their leftovers. What else do they have up there, Assaf? I see many supplies coming and going. Is there anything else today?"

"I didn't have a chance to ask, but yesterday the blond one said they would share everything with us, maybe candy later. I will check again after school, Ima," he answered her gently and then leaned over to kiss her, pleased that she allowed him this show of affection; normally she shied away from even a quick hug.

*

When I was eight, wars and daring soldiers were the stuff of television shows and movies I disliked watching. I had a lot of time to watch television at Eshkol's where my father worked. He was the new manager of the large television store.

There you could bring in every kind of television that had ever existed, practically obsolete black-and- whites, gleaming polished new ones that still smelled like Styrofoam from the delivery boxes, portable ones as small as lunch pails.

You could repair your television set, trade it in, or sell it. The shop was in a commercial area of town called G. H. It was one long line of fast food restaurants: McDonald's, Dairy Queen, Wendy's, and Burger King. In between there were independently owned shops that sold shoes, household objects, clothing, and there was also Eshkol's TV Repairs and Sales.

Eshkol was a last name, but no one seemed to know his first name. He had bald-in-the-front hair; what a lipstick or eye shadow today might be called, burnt-orange color. His high, white, creased forehead and his thick, brown glasses dominated his face and he had no other distinguishing facial features, no beard or moustache.

A black, leather motorcycle jacket, his only distinctive article of clothing. I can't tell you if he was tall or short, fat or thin, but he was probably none of those things or my mother would have mentioned it to me enough times that I would remember. She has a habit of referring to people by weight and height that is out of fashion.

"Which one? You mean the daughter? Oh, she was always big, even as a girl. What can you do? The guy who came to fix the windows? God he was tall. People say Jews aren't tall, but my own cousin was six foot four. But who remembers? He's been gone so long. What a waste."

Next door to Eshkol's was a children's hair dressing salon. There were *Sesame Street* drawings on the walls. Big Bird smiling down at Ernie and Bert, Cookie Monster with a plate full of crumbs, his blue, furry cheeks bulging.

A large, paved parking lot encircled the shop and Eshkol's cherry-red motorcycle was always parked outside the front glass door. The door had a bell attached to it which announced each entry. Inside the shop it was large and spacious, and humming with the muted sounds of TV. You entered into a thinly carpeted showroom full of the latest television sets.

The most prestigious was an Electrolux, but there were many large floor models with chestnut wood paneling. As you went farther in there was the repair area: long, dirty, and narrow. Middle-aged Jewish men with names like Syd and Saul were bent over dusty television tubes, twisting around different colored wiring with miniature screwdrivers.

Calendars depicting plastic smiling women in strapless or low cut tops and tight jean or elastic-waist shorts hung on nails jammed into the walls. Backless television sets covered most of the available space except the inches occupied by black saucer-like ashtrays and coffee cups that always had cigarette ash mixed in with the dregs.

The repairmen taught me how to vacuum out the thick dust from the maze of wires at the back of a TV, how to put the tubes in the tester to see if they still worked or needed replacing. A third section of the shop was partitioned off with glass walls. It was the office for calculating payments and receipts. There were three black telephones on the large desk. The kind with round dials and the phone number of the shop written in blue ink in the center. There was also an answering machine, a gray filing cabinet, and a wastepaper basket.

A wide flight of stained, carpeted stairs led to the basement I knew was as large as the upstairs. I never went down there because it emanated foreign, off-putting smells. The air changed, thickened, as you lowered yourself onto the first step, which I sometimes did half-jokingly, already panic-stricken at my childish daring. Your lungs suddenly seemed threatened, in danger of closing, as though there was an invisible wall between the first and second floor.

My father told me that Eshkol was divorced and he lived downstairs. His ex-wife lived in a camping trailer nearby, and they were still friends. He cautioned me not to go downstairs with the tilt of his head and the lifting of his black eyebrows when he saw me place my sneakers on the first step.

I had learned at a young age how to read my father's rippling body language and wide-eyed facial expressions in much the same way as I imagine my father had internalized the meaning of his own father's small movements, his voice.

*

"Nomi!"

All three of them jumped at father's customary bark. Father wears the clothing of his socialist political party, *Mapai*. Loyal *Mapainiks* wear khaki from head to toe, Shabbat and weekdays. He always adds his dusty gray hat to this uniform, never a *kippah*. Assaf thought he had gone to work.

"Do you know what happened to me today?" Father growls. "I was expecting my promotion. Went in early. That promotion was for me. In my hand."

Three sets of eyes stare down at the cold stone floor. Even at seven, Adi knows better than to look up. His cereal-covered spoon hangs between his fingers. Now the dysa will be cold.

"Do you know what they did? The *mamzerim*! Do you know what they did? They brought in this Russian Jew, some Ashkenazi from Russia. He doesn't know the first thing. The first thing he does not know. They gave him the position and then they asked me, me who has been working, no, slaving for a decade and a half for them, an honest to God slave I have been, they asked me to teach him the ropes. Can you believe that?"

Father's black eyes are exploding like the small pieces of shrapnel bursting on Ben Yehudah Street. Sharp and jagged. He is clean-shaven and he has smooth, spotless, desk-job hands. He glares at his wife. Finally, she looks up.

"Well, that's your party," she spits at him in Arabic. "Your party whose behinds you kiss day and night. What do you think? You're a token, Mordechai. You know? One Kurdi, one Parsi, one Moroccai, and one Temani. You went up a little, but no more. You'll never go up more. That's your party," she repeats.

Assaf can see her shoulders tense, and he knows her feet are ready. His own toes twitch inside his shoes.

"Silence!" Mordechai snarls and lunges for her at the same time.

But she is too fast for him, too prepared. She dives into the next room and quickly hops onto the balcony; her most common escape route. The brothers hear her pounding feet on the stone path that leads to the green iron gate at the end of the garden. Soon she will be cursing her husband over fresh doughy *saluf* dipped in *hilbeh* with her girlfriend, Mazal. Mazal feels sorry for her.

Father returns from the balcony. He breathes heavily. He is young, healthy, and has never smoked, but luckily for his wife, he was never a good runner. Tears spill onto the floor and Assaf remembers his little brother, Adi.

"Don't worry. I will stay here until Ima gets back. I won't leave you alone. Come Adi, finish the dysa."

"It's cold now."

"I will heat it up for you outside on the fire. Come."

I knew that in the center of their living room stood a kerosene heater, called a primos. My father told me it was their only source of heat until they bought an oven, but by then he'd become a soldier. Besides, kerosene was rationed along with all other necessary supplies in Jerusalem.

"He is not alone. He has school now, no time to heat baby food. Get to work. You'll be late. What will you be later on, the way you are about studies?"

"I don't want to go anyhow. I hate it. Why do you want me to go so much? You just said the Ashkenazim didn't give you the job you wanted. Why do you push me toward them?"

"You will learn something there, that's why. What do the Temanim learn at school? They have nothing. The teachers don't know much more than the students. Go."

He said this last word in a tone that made my father understand; if he doesn't get going his father will simply start barking unstoppably like the wild dog they keep tied outside in the back of the garden to scare the Arabs away. That was before the war, before the Arabs in the nearby villages fled, abandoning their homes seemingly overnight.

Adi grabs his brother's arm, but Assaf shakes it off gently and goes. It is finally spring, maybe he can start cleaning people's yards and save enough money to buy a bicycle.

"Hey Assaf! You're late, too? I will walk with you until my school. My mother didn't want to let me go today. She heard too much bombing in the night. It's quieter now, so I begged her to let me go, otherwise, she'd have me feeding chickens and searching for wild herbs and grasses in the fields all day. I hear on *kibbutzim* they have real fruits and vegetables, maybe we should go there."

It is Moshiko, his best friend. He is half skipping half flying down the narrow sidewalk, with a worn-out *siddur* under one arm and a small piece of newspaper stuffed into his front pocket. Inside is flat, brown pita stuffed with hard-boiled egg. Assaf notices it and realizes that he has nothing for lunch again.

"*B'emet?* You beg to go to school. I wish I could go to your school. I swear if that teacher twists my ear today, I will grow up to burn his house down."

"*Misken* you are. To *gehenom* with those white Jews, worse than the Arabs. Don't worry. Next year you will be bar mitzvah, after that you can leave that awful place and come with the rest of us to school. Your father won't be able to control you after thirteen. Besides, we're going to make money. I'm learning how to fix engines. Motorcycles, cars, anything. I'll teach you."

"You'll teach me," Assaf repeats. "*Beseder*, my friend."

My grandmother has probably returned from Mazal's tiny kitchen. Perhaps she's putting on her cleaning-lady clothes, a dreadfully patched, blue skirt and matching top.

A bomb explodes, but Moshiko and Assaf walk on. It isn't close enough to stop and look for cover. The ground does not jump beneath their feet. Not yet.

"Hey? There's one of our small planes. Do you think they will let me practice on the engines a little? Use their tools?" Moshiko asked.

"We can ask them. My house has become the new Jewish border of Jerusalem," Assaf answers. He does not try to disguise his pride.

"Your father, he doesn't care about the airport?"

"They promised to pay him after the war. You should have seen how they leveled the field. *Chik chak*. Nothing for them. They share everything with us. Come over later and see."

They arrive at the corner where Moshiko turns off; for Assaf there is another kilometer and a half to go.

Father does not return home that night. Although it has never happened before, no one glances at the heavy iron gate or mentions his name.

"Go up to the roof and give some fresh eggs to the soldiers."

That's all Mother says the entire evening, while she boils wild grass in the week's water ration. They will use whatever water is left in the pot for the dirty dishes, which they assemble and clean in one bucket and the remaining drops for the toilet.

Assaf does not go up to the roof until Moshiko arrives. A red-headed soldier shows the boys an airplane engine. The cigarette smoke fills the air and coffee flows on the roof endlessly, like the British soldiers on their Sunday marches under the Occupation.

"Hey, your eyes are red, *atah beseder?*" Chaim asks Assaf. He is one of the soldiers in charge of the airport.

"It's just the smoke," he answers, half grinning.

"Have a piece of chocolate."

His hand is warm. Assaf feels him slip a square of chocolate into the pocket of his tight, faded jacket. Moshiko's head is buried in an airplane engine, but Assaf promises himself he will share the rare treat with him later.

As dawn breaks, the chickens wake the boys as usual and Assaf is the first to force himself out of bed and head for the washroom. They are the only ones on the street with an indoor toilet and bath. The rest of the crowded road uses outhouses and the public bathhouse once a week.

Another day passes with no sign of Father. Mother's face relaxes a little. Maybe he has disappeared like the British patrols and their vicious dogs that never drooled on their polished black boots.

After school, the boys help Mother. They slice hard prickly *sabras*, the only fruit growing wild in Jerusalem. There is a knock at the iron gate.

"A policeman came. It's your father. He's in the hospital," Mother tells them when she returns down the stone path. The only hospital is run by nuns.

"His leg is broken; shrapnel from a bomb. He was so furious when he left here about the promotion. He probably just galloped off to work like a donkey and thought himself invisible in the center of town, in the middle of a war."

Mother could have been discussing the squashed *juke* she found on the bottom of her shapeless shoe in the morning, or the time Mazal accidentally tore the wedding dress she had preserved all the way from Yemen for her seven daughters. She could never be sentimental about a wedding dress, even one that is not her own.

An explosion erupts in Assaf's mind and he remembers the bomb that exploded the day before on his way to school.

"You have to go to the hospital to visit him after school tomorrow," she continues quietly.

The sound of the bomb is still between the boy's ears. It had not seemed threateningly close. Sometimes only one landed and then there was time before another one. Time enough to get to a bomb shelter. Sometimes many landed one after the other and there wasn't much time. The friends had dug their hands deeper into their pockets and suddenly their shoulders were touching, but they kept on walking. Assaf wondered if he should save money for a bicycle, which would lengthen the life of his shoes, or if he should buy shoes he could run fast in.

"Assaf, you must promise me you will go. He still has the paycheck from *Mapai* in his pocket. If you don't visit him, he won't give us anything."

"I have to go to a school I hate. I have to go to a hospital. I don't want to see him."

"The soldiers won't be on the roof forever. Who knows how long? There is little need for cleaners during a war maybe."

She stops there and her hard, brown eyes catch his and he cannot look away.

"Okay, beseder, Ima."

Before the sun sets the sky is a rich, cloudless blue, the airplanes are still visible. Assaf looks up and spots two. They are flying low and he knows in minutes they will land in the field behind his home, then the weary pilots will climb the ladder up to his roof for some lukewarm water or a cup of hot coffee.

The faint purr of the engines overhead comforts him. He is curious about the red-headed soldier; is he one of the pilots in the sky now and what supplies is he carrying today? Powdered eggs and powdered milk or bullets and rifles?

*

Eshkol's was something I had forgotten about, like the pilots my father met on his roof as a boy during Israel's first war. Then one day my mother was exhausted from showing off my new son. We were visiting Ottawa from Israel and she had organized a lavish Shabbat tea. Some of her old friends I remembered and others were strangers. There was one woman who was fond of my baby; she had trouble returning him.

"You don't remember her?" my mother asked me afterward, as she filled her outstretched palm with the crumbs she was sweeping off the table with her other hand. "Well, I guess you wouldn't."

Then she laughed girlishly; like we were friends at a sleepover, not mother and daughter. I felt a kind of gaiety surge through her like it made her touch her youth again to think about it. Afterward, this surprised me as I would have expected something closer to a look of disgust and a shake of the head, as though turning away from a close-up view of roadkill while sitting in the passenger seat.

"Abba, why did you hang out with these guys? How could you work for someone like Eshkol?" I asked him after the conversation with my mother. I couldn't stop thinking about the woman at the tea, holding my baby and cooing.

"Hang out, shmang out. What does it mean to hang out? Eshkol, he was downstairs, he gave me his shop to run. That's how I paid the mortgage, the bills, you think your mother could care less about bills? Visa's calling me, not her. What do I care what *drek* is downstairs? They were all dopies, dummies, why God makes them I don't know, but he makes them. Me? I made money with the TVs. It was good money all right. At least he didn't give me to clean floors like the Canadian Jews when I asked them for a job."

"He made porno movies down there—of himself and all of his girlfriends, including his Jewish ex-wives. She was his first wife. No *children*." My mother emphasized the word children. "He used to take out Jewish girls, get them drunk and take them down there. Before they knew what was happening, he was filming himself with these women. Reels and reels. Think of it, they're old ladies like her now. Then he'd invite a bunch of guys downstairs; they'd drink and do God knows what and watch. He used to watch himself with these women for hours. Oh, he was something I tell you. He was a real..."

She stopped reminiscing and looked into my green and gold flecked eyes. I looked directly back into her identical pair. Perhaps she was waiting for my reaction or maybe she was worried about these revelations, about how they reflected on her.

Pita for Two

"Your mother must have told you something about me and Anat?" Yoel asks. He looks injured; a scrape with tiny holes of warm blood leaking through the skin.

In my ten years in Israel I have been careful not to mention Yoel and Anat in the same breath. Looking at his thin, youthful face, his fashionable goatee and sideburns, and stylish clothing, I have to remind myself that he is my father's first cousin.

He does have my father's identical carob-colored, smooth Yemenite skin. Long, lean, narrow, dressed in appropriately faded jeans and a tight, black T-shirt, he is the only relative I know in Israel.

Yoel lives in Tel Aviv, an hour's bus ride away, but he comes as often as once a week for a visit. My father is shorter, five foot ten, with a broad back that suits his muscular stomach, arms, and legs. His moustache is as much a part of him as his wide nose and the gold tooth he has on the right side of his mouth. There are no jeans in my father's wardrobe and T-shirts are only useful for exercising or fixing things around the house; shirts with buttons reveal the strong chest underneath.

I pull weeds out of the lawn around the edges. My husband has no time for the garden and gardeners are expensive in my neighborhood. My cousin tends his garden in Tel Aviv so deftly, I think mine may distract him.

"You should give that palm more water," Yoel says, motioning to the tree in the right-hand corner, next to the empty space where the built-in barbeque is supposed to be. I smile, hoping that he will not expect an answer.

"I told her to take all of the furniture, anything electrical, I don't care about them. *Aht yoda'at*, Miri, we own another small apartment at the entrance to Tel Aviv. 'Tell the man we can't give him more time and take it,' I said. Liat and Yonatan already told me they want to live with me."

He seems disfigured somehow, deflated; an ill blow-up doll who has slowly been leaking the contents of its stomach all morning, its insides emptied out all over my lawn, still yellow from the winter. Sapped of his usual energy, he unfolds an outdoor blanket on the grass and flops down.

His spread-out arms and legs remind me of when I was a girl in Ottawa; my brother and I lying flat on our backs, making snow angels by sweeping our arms and legs back and forth across the frozen ground.

We used to rush outside to make as many as we could before the school bus arrived, before a dog or neighbor had time to mess up the perfect sheets of white that had fallen from the sky while we slept.

I go inside to check on my baby. She is in the same spot as she was when I put her down. Returning to the garden, I lie on my stomach beside my cousin, who seems to have dozed off in the embrace of the winter sun. My garden is still in the mid-afternoon. The children are at school and there is little traffic here in the Judaean hills, between Jerusalem and Tel Aviv.

I was grateful that my cousin was too tired to continue talking about his marriage. It was his childhood that fascinated me, the parts of his childhood that brushed my father's youth. I gave up asking him to tell me about it when he told me he has no memory of the British soldiers with their polished boots, their starched uniforms and no recollection of the war, the hundreds of bombs that exploded half a mile from his home.

"All I know, Mirileh," he said putting his hand on my knee, as he often does, "is that when I was a little boy your father's parents took me in, right before they divorced, right after my parents were...." He stops there.

Aside from the subject of Anat, I never ask Yoel about the car accident that killed his parents. I am not even sure if it was a car accident or something else. Yoel refuses to talk about it, like my father.

I nod and look down until Yoel continues "In spite of all of her troubles, your grandmother took me in when no one else would. I like to think that I helped her, too, that she did not want to be completely alone and your big father was in the army, the paratroopers and Moshe and Shmuli were gone to the kibbutz, even before Shmuli's bar mitzvah."

Yoel had lived alone with my grandmother, Nomi, in the stone house in Jerusalem, and now, the loneliness that occupied him as a child had reappeared. His own children were out of high school, his wife had turned a linen closet into a tiny bedroom of her own, and Yoel remains, tending his garden just as my grandmother did throughout her depression half a century ago.

My grandmother's garden was not lush like Yoel's modern one, but mostly sand and stone except for the roses she enjoyed growing. Yoel told me she picked them every Friday for the neighbors, the *shul*, the *havdalah* spices, the smelling of which separated the Sabbath from the rest of the week.

It was not Yoel who had pointed out the large, square, black roof of my father's childhood home to me, I read about it in a book. The roof still looked freshly tarred and flattened from its time as a makeshift control tower for the fledgling Israeli air force.

My sister's mother-in-law, Chana, grew up down the road from my father's family and for her seventieth birthday she self-published a short novel to celebrate her life. She gave one copy to each family member as a keepsake.

The neighborhood of her childhood is described in detail, including the small airplanes that landed in the field, a stone's throw away from what was once my father's back door. These mostly single-engine planes flew desperately needed supplies into besieged Jerusalem. I came across the novel by chance when I was poring over my sister's bookshelves one day, and she had not batted an eye when I asked her if I could take it home.

All of the questions I had ever asked Yoel about his childhood had been met with the same answer *"Ani lo zocher*, I don't remember. I was too little." These protests were accompanied by a large shrug of his shoulders and a smile that begged me to talk of the merciless sun, the incomprehensible government, the cost of a round trip bus ticket from Tel Aviv to Jerusalem, anything but what I wanted to know.

I spent hours translating the first half of Chana's book, written in simple Hebrew, into English. Her story blended with fragments my father told me as a child and bits I heard my mother whisper into the receiver. I combined this information with what I could glean from the look on Yoel's face as he raised his shoulders to his ears and offered me a pastry, stuffed with fresh apples that he had schlepped all the way to the Jerusalem *shuk* to purchase, or another Nescafé. I tried to reconstruct Yoel's childhood, a childhood forever running more than a decade behind my father's.

My cousin appears exposed with his limbs spread wide in the grass in my garden. Probably as vulnerable as he had looked as a schoolboy, standing in the shuk, with the smell of freshly baked rolls and warm, white sugar making his mouth water, as he digs his hands deeper into his empty pockets.

There was nothing to eat for breakfast. His stomach growls and he bows his head in shame. My grandmother, Nomi, is in bed, sick for two days now. She keeps telling him that she needs only to rest, but he notices that she sleeps little.

Instead she stares at the ceiling, rubbing her slight bones from time to time. Sometimes she lies still with cold, sliced cucumbers over her eyelids or soggy teabags. A glass full of *hilbeh* mixed with water sits on the cement block that acts as her side table. She takes small reluctant sips of the drink, and it seems to help her relax.

"For my stomach," she says to Yoel, smiling weakly. "Why don't you go to school?" she asks him, even if it is four o'clock in the morning.

Nomi has been unable to work as a cleaner for weeks. Yoel could not recall how many. My father told me that my grandmother's pregnancies had damaged her eyesight and her hearing, that the doctor had advised her to stop having children after her first, although she had gone on to bear three more sons and take in a fourth.

The last pregnancy left her as her doctor had predicted, but she was divorced by then, and she needed to feed herself and Yoel. When she was not strong enough to clean homes, she sat in the front yard and baked *saluf* for passers-by.

For many tourists these spiced pitas were a novelty and she normally earned enough for at least one filling meal a day for both of them, sometimes two. They already had fresh eggs to eat from the chickens, and there was never any rent to pay. My grandfather, Mordechai, had purchased the small, stone house outright as soon as he and Nomi became engaged.

*

"But what did you do when your mother couldn't work? How could your father work so close to your home and never stop by to see Yoel?" I asked my father.

I had phoned him to say Chana wrote a book about her childhood and I was the unofficial translator.

"Him? He was happy the divorce came before his own son, Shmuli's bar mitzvah. So, you think he will be worried about an orphan not even related through blood? Do you know what was Yoel's bar mitzvah? Nothing. I tried to help them, but there was a war going on with Egypt and it was not easy for me to get out. She was tired all the time, her muscles hurt. I came with a shade for her to put over the garden, a big black one, but when you're sick, you know? The heat, it gives you a headache. She was proud and embarrassed to look weak. She looked more at the chickens than at us, especially Yoel. He never likes to talk about it."

There was a long pause while I digested that; while I tried to connect my father's words with Yoel's generous smile.

"Hey. We're talking long distance. Don't waste your money, Miri. I'll write you a letter."

My father hung up before I had a chance to respond, but I knew a letter would be coming in the mail, written on both sides and in all the margins in his beautiful Hebrew script. In English my father still forgets to insert vowels, no matter how many times I remind him that vowels might be optional in Hebrew, but only spies write English without them.

My garden is really an extension of the playroom; the deflated baby pool has blown into a corner and caught on the struggling honeysuckle, an infant swing with a broken safety belt hangs from the pergola, and there are broken pieces of dolls' heads the dog has dragged outside by the hair.

It is a world apart from Yoel's garden. He spends hours on a Friday enticing the purples, pinks and oranges to blossom, forming archways of white bougainvilleas like wedding canopies across the entrance, filling old bathtubs with green cacti and rich, black soil. I imagine he sometimes longs for the little shul across the road from the home he shared with my grandmother.

It is still there, the roses still accepted for havdalah on Saturday nights, he tells me. He knows because he sometimes brings them in from Tel Aviv. It must be impossible for Yoel to care for his garden without hearing my grandmother's voice. So soon after he'd lost one mother, his second one began deteriorating before his eyes.

"Shoo! Out of here!" I hear Nomi exclaiming, clapping her hands sharply and clicking her tongue against the roof of her mouth, a stern expression on her wrinkled brown face. "You're messing up my dough!" she scolds the rooster, as she looks for a higher flat stone to rest the dough upon.

Her thick, long, black braid, streaked with gray hairs is wound tightly on the top of her head. She covers her head with a thin, satin scarf the color of rain clouds or midnight black. If one scarf is on her head Yoel knows the other is soaking in a basin of warm water and flakey, sand-colored soap. His aunt is scrupulously clean.

The last couple of days Nomi had not even tried to rise from her narrow wooden bed, and with Assaf in the army Yoel never knows when he is coming home. It could be tomorrow or in two months. In the meantime, they need to eat. His other cousins, Moshe and Shmuli never come home. They moved to a kibbutz in the center of the country and they have forgotten about them, like their father.

*

Bright red tomatoes, shiny green cucumbers, sweet yellow apples, fresh fragrant apricots and ripening lemons; I know the Jerusalem market and you can practically taste each fruit as you pass through the aisles.

For Yoel it would have been the same, the market hasn't changed that much in five decades. It still opens at seven in the morning, the bakeries even earlier and the farmers' voices ring out clear and clean: "Tomatoes the best and the cheapest, apricots come take a look, take a look and try mine!"

In the fifties nobody would have directed their eyes toward Yoel. He was tall for his age and his thinness probably made him look even taller. His dark skin and black hair were clean and smooth, but ten-year-olds were not preferred customers, and with such dark features, who knows? He could be an Arab boy waiting to snatch a melon or a few unwatched coins.

Yoel knew how to get food for himself and his aunt. My father had told him over and over again: "Help Doda, okay, Yoeli? My Abba's gone now and he has a new wife. Don't wait for him, he is gone. Help Doda when you see I'm not around. Don't worry about school. Trust me. It's a waste of time."

Doda shouldn't have to clean floors and toilets. It wasn't right, especially when she wasn't feeling well, how could the little boy, who is still so sensitive, help but think? Yoel often came to the large Jerusalem market to help his aunt, just like Assaf had told him. Assaf was a paratrooper and Yoel was full of admiration for him in his ironed khaki uniform and candy-red beret.

Assaf explained to him how candy-red meant he jumped out of airplanes. He spent countless early mornings among rows of fruits and vegetables, but often he never saw them. Instead, he saw his powerful cousin sliding down from his big, black polished Harley-Davidson and taking off in a soaring airplane with a parachute on his muscular shoulders, falling through the airy sky in his handsome uniform.

When I feel I will lose my nerve; when I had to pass my Israeli driving test; board a local bus with a newborn in my arms after a recent bombing, I cling to my father's image too. *Don't be so weak, Canadian. Be strong like me, not afraid of nobody.*

The Jerusalem market is a busy place. It could not have taken more than a quarter of an hour for Yoel to spot her; a middle-aged woman, alone, juggling three bags of overflowing groceries, mostly heavy vegetables and fruits. Perfect.

"*Slichah, Giveret.* Can I help you?" he asks, trotting over to the tall blond woman.

"Thanks, sweetie," Karina replied beaming down at him. Yoel thought she looked so friendly, she might bend over and kiss him. He took a step back. She did not notice and continued chatting, "I was just thinking, what am I going to do with so much stuff? My shopping cart broke this morning. The wheel just rolled right down the street and on to who knows where and instead of buying a new one right away I thought, well I am having a dinner party, I'll just have to manage. And look? Even a boy sees I can't manage," she lowered her bags to the ground, brushed her thick, straight hair out of her eyes and laughed.

"Aren't you lucky for me? A lucky charm!"

My cousin would have been too shy to respond beyond a grin, even today in the face of Anat's bitterness, he inhales every syllable without allowing himself to retaliate beyond his familiar shrugs and sighs. It is easy to picture him bending down, taking the two heaviest bags in his arms and following the stranger across the street.

To ignore the hunger pains in his stomach maybe he tried to focus on the graceful movement of Karina's long, bare legs, or the strange happy song she was likely singing under her breath.

Yoel told me he spent his teenage years living in Jerusalem's Russian Quarter. Karina must have lived on one of those narrow streets. It was easy to understand how a child would have been mesmerized by Karina's blond light after so much darkness; the jazzy tunes she probably hummed absently, the graceful dance steps she performed along the thin sidewalk.

No doubt he had the sudden urge to laugh out loud, but he would have been careful not to; Yoel is always conscious of embarrassing others. Most likely he sucked in his cheeks and focused on the pavement.

"Don't you like jazz?" she might have asked, when they finally stopped in front of a small house, one in a crowded row. The morning sunshine makes the ageing Jerusalem stone walls look new and polished. Karina's front door looked like the entrance to a stone cave, except it was painted baby blue, even the frame was blue. I once saw some of Yoel's watercolors and he had painted her apartment in varying shades of blue.

My cousin is a collector, not just paintings; European ceramic bowls as large as fruit baskets and as small as teacups decorate entire walls, all the way to the ceiling. A whole series of African masks stare eyeless at anyone attempting to eat at the kitchen table, coffee spoons, mostly from Israeli-Arab markets, line the passage leading to the bathroom.

When he saw me looking at his artwork, he snatched the pile away with an uncharacteristic grab. Dumbfounded, I met his gaze. The paintings had been lying openly on the kitchen table. He quickly put on a thin smile and offered to pick geraniums in the garden for my tea, but I had read the titles: "Karina 1956" and "Morning at Studio Entrance."

Now I had Yoel's own creations to help me conjure up the stories of his childhood I wanted to know so badly. I could fill in the spaces anyway I wanted. On the blue background a gold saxophone lies on top of a black, grand piano.

A pretty blond woman rests on her stomach across the top of the piano, her bare legs, crossed at the ankles, were up in the air, her white arms folded under her chin. She looks as though she is giggling at a joke someone had just told her, perhaps the painter.

Is that how Karina looked? Her cheerful voice must have been irresistible to an orphaned boy, abandoned by his uncle, living with no one but an ill aunt, and stray chickens.

"How old are you boy? Eleven? Twelve?"

"Ten."

"Well, then I don't suppose you would like jazz. Wait here and I will pay you for being such a sweetie."

Yoel must have watched, fascinated by her every movement as Karina took a key out of a small purse and placed it into the lock. He noticed a sign above the door. In clear black Hebrew letters it read: *Karina's Dance Studio since 1950. Ballet, Jazz, Tap for all ages.*

Underneath there was more writing, but Yoel couldn't be sure of the languages. Russian? German? There were Jews from all over the world in Jerusalem. He knew that because he often watched as strangers photographed my grandmother baking pitas. Afterward they often asked him questions, or offered to pay him and he had been unable to grasp a word.

A hungry boy surely wondered who had time for dancing when it took up so much time to find money for food and clothing. Even after the rabbis finally forced my grandfather to leave, a year before Yoel met Karina, my grandmother didn't dance, not even on holidays or at weddings.

I once overheard my father discussing his mother in an unusually quiet voice with Yoel on one of his Ottawa visits. My father said his mother might have been different if the divorce had come ten years earlier, she might have felt light enough to dance. Instead she had chained herself to her bitterness. I could tell Yoel did not fully understand my father's words. How could he? Ten years before the divorce he barely existed.

Karina must have understood Yoel's poverty. She probably gave him a couple of lirot and a pastry ringed with chocolate from one of her bags.

From Yoel's painting of her you can imagine a woman who smells of flowery perfume and faintly of havdalah wine. Her sundress was a maze of small white polka dots on a lavender background. It had spaghetti straps and a low back. She looked tangible and I wanted to touch her pretty yellow hair, her soft pink cheeks and matching lips.

"Such a polite boy! You had better get to school before it's too late," I could hear her remark. Yoel had remembered to paint her red nails, her shiny salmon coral rings and twin bracelets.

In every photo I had ever seen of my grandmother she wore no jewelry and she was dressed in dark colors: gray, brown, navy, black. Yoel had never had a sister or a living grandmother. I do not know how much he recalled of his own mother. At school there was a gentle, withered, old rabbi, who seemed to be talking to himself as much as the students, at least that's how Yoel had always described school.

Even this detail I gleaned only after plaguing him with questions. He must have longed to linger in her apartment, to wait around for a second pastry. But Karina had a business to run; she was a woman on her own in the Middle East. She needed to go.

I imagine Yoel as a boy with his ear to the cold steel door; his cheek resting on the picture of the pretty blond woman, right on her cheek. Karina singing the same cheerful unfamiliar song she had been singing all the way home from the market, only this time in his head. I had never been to the Russian Quarter in my many long walks around Jerusalem with my cousin, but I burned to ask him: Do you ever go there now?

*

It was no longer warm outside, but the cool air did not disturb my cousin's slumber. He worked shifts and sometimes double shifts at the hospital. Soon my children would return from school and be thrilled to see him. My oldest was only seven, too young to make wild guesses about others. I guessed Yoel was gay when I was twelve.

One Shabbat after shul I returned home to find my mother reclining on her side of the couch, the side no one dared to sit in, even when she wasn't home. She was staring at the turned-off television, which was always switched on immediately in our house on weekdays before anyone found a light. Although he was married, Yoel was visiting alone from Israel.

"Mom?"

"Yes, Miri?"

"Mom, is Yoel gay?" I said it straight out, like I had once asked, don't all sinners go to hell, after a discussion about the next world in Hebrew school.

My mother opened her mouth and closed it a few times, like a child playing in front of a mirror; trying to choose a face. She continued to gaze at the blank television screen while I waited.

"How did you know that?" she asked, but her words came out slowly, like the last drops of medicine in an upside-down bottle.

"I don't know," I answered honestly. "I looked at him today and I knew."

"Don't mention it to your father, please. Okay? He loves his cousin like a brother, but he hates gays."

"Well, he is married. How can that—? "

"Miri, that's enough" she snapped. She was fingering the blue Star of David that always adorned her neck and I wondered if she was doing it purposely.

"Now, we won't ever have to tell you."

It was obvious that the subject was closed. She turned back to the lifeless television screen, while I wondered if God hated gays like my father did and how Anat, who smelled like tuna fish and lemon juice, could be married to a man who preferred men.

My mother and I never discussed it again and my father only mentioned his feelings about homosexuality once to me. I am sure he has forgotten. It was after he had returned home from the weekly square dance club he had agreed to join to "make your mother happy."

My father is a man who is either under the body of a car or under a bench press in his makeshift gym in our basement. He is suitable for Sunday afternoon tag team wrestling; not Sunday night square dancing.

"Everyone from our shul goes," my mother would sing, as soon as the clock struck 7:30 on those nights. The square dance caller took up his post at 8:00. She donned her dancing costume like a child on Purim, with fresh excitement. My father looked at it differently.

"They go out and square dance for an hour," he began the morning after opening night. "Then over greasy French fries and fried hot dogs over at Levi's, they congratulate themselves on how much exercise they're getting. I just sit there with my black coffee and say nothing. What do they know about exercise?"

My father straightened his broad back as he spoke; emphasizing his muscular chest and shoulders. He added more granola into his plain yogurt and stirred it until it was evenly mixed.

"You know what I hate most? You have to hold hands with men! Their hands are all sweaty and we have to keep changing partners. I like to lift weights not touching nobody."

He looked like a man with a mouth full of eggshells had just run up and kissed him on the mouth. He stopped chewing.

It was not my father, but Yoel who was the dancer in the family, my mother still laments; she adores him.

"You should see your cousin dance!" she said to me many times when I was growing up. "He danced all over Europe in his twenties," she added. "He learned English and French from ballerinas."

"Ballerinas? Boy ones?" I remember asking her, but she didn't respond to that. "Not like your father. He never offers to take me dancing. Only when your cousin visits do I get to go out and move around a bit. He knows how to dance with a woman."

It seemed bizarre to me at the time. How could my father who had to walk miles to school in torn shoes, sleep outdoors with farm animals when his father was angry enough, and chop olive branches for heat have come from the same home as a cousin who speaks two European languages, paints and dances?

"He was a baby when I was already married, Miri," was all my father offered when I asked. "It was not the same for him, and besides, he had a few years with his own parents; who knows what they taught him?"

When I questioned Yoel about how he learned to move so gracefully, he told me that he once lived with an artist, but I never knew that she had fed him, clothed him, took him in like a bird who had headed straight for a glass wall. So, on balance my father and his baby cousin weren't so different.

The thoughts padding back and forth across Yoel's young mind were like the rabbi's ruler at school, sliding back and forth across the ancient Hebrew letters. On one hand, his shoulders ached from lifting baskets brimming with fruits and vegetables.

On the other hand, he had his cousin's proud eyes boring into his own. Should he leave his aunt to work for Karina? Could he do this to the broken woman who had taken him in? This must have been his quandary. I try to imagine the scene, how it was when the decision was final.

"Yoel!" Karina exclaims, as she opens her door wide later that afternoon. "Breakfast is quite a ways away. Did you forget something?"

Karina is wearing a cream-colored body suit and nude tights or maybe baby pink. At the wrists of the tight, long sleeves are three identical rows of shiny blue sequins. On her feet are black tap shoes with small black bows in the center. They look brand new. Embarrassed, Yoel lowers his gaze. His pockets fill with his hands, his blush is hot.

"It is rare that handsome boys coming knocking at my door after *siesta* time," Karina says delicately. "Please come in."

Yoel enters and Karina disappears. When she returns, she is wearing a soft pink robe over her dancing outfit.

"I was just doing some warm-ups when I heard you knocking. I have a class to teach in half an hour. Would you like a drink of water and some cookies or fruit?"

"Yes, umm, no. I would like to talk about something first."

"First eat. It is good for strength and muscles. Then talk."

Yoel smiles and allows his body to be led into the cozy kitchen. His arm shakes still; Karina held his hand. Her slim, white fingers were warm and soft like his aunt's fresh pitas on the wide flat stones in his garden. It is hard for him to concentrate on what she is saying, but he is conscious of her high-pitched laughter, like the sound the teapot makes when it is just about to boil.

To avoid staring at her strong bare legs, Yoel keeps his eyes on the tiled floor. The tiles are a salmon color and remind him of a flower his aunt grows in the garden, but at this moment he cannot remember its name. He is conscious of putting one foot in front of the other. Right, left, right, left. This stops his knees from trembling. Had he become a beggar?

*

My grandmother would have been unaware of Yoel's new relationship. Even I know about the unspoken pact between Yoel and my father: change only upsets her, she's suffered enough. She spent most afternoons in the front yard, sifting flour for fresh batches of *saluf*.

This I had heard often enough, even from my mother. She must have been grateful when morning gave way to afternoon and the cool breezes began. Her joints swelled up in the heat, and her ankles became so large she could not fit into her shoes; at forty-five she seemed like an old *safta*.

"I remember waking up in the night and touching her skin. She was freezing, Miri. Frozen really," my father told me when I asked him if they had family doctors in those days. "My father was snoring to wake the dead, as usual. What did he care? There wasn't a single blanket in the house that night. I covered her with my own body until dawn. I slept on her legs. Then I went to get the doctor. He knew her a long time already and knew what she needed. He gave her some shot, something. I don't know what, but she felt better. In the morning my father had no idea what happened. When I told him, he shouted at me: Did you keep the bill? Don't you know I can't claim the money back from medical aide without a receipt? This is all he cared about, that he shouldn't have to pay for the home visit. *Mamzer echad.*"

Still a mother, my grandmother must have wondered when Yoel was going to come home from school. She couldn't seem to remember from one day to the next if he came home at 2:00 or 4:00, or even later. She began to lose her short-term memory young.

She knew he rose with the chickens because the house was always tidy when she arrived in the kitchen each morning and she woke up early enough. Even if she was too tired to wash up the dishes from the night before, the sink was spotless.

Lately Yoel had been leaving breakfast out for her. I doubt my grandmother asked him where he was suddenly getting the money to buy food daily; God was the true source of all provisions.

Karina must have gone to see my grandmother herself. Yoel would never have stopped coming back to her. Years after his aunt was found dead, my own mother told me how he had banged his head against his bedroom door until it bled.

"Miri, I tell you I thought he was never going to stop. I can still hear him screaming, Ima! Ima! as though it were his own mother all over again. And the blood running into his eyes. God!"

Karina must have known when Yoel came home from school. Perhaps she followed him. I imagine Nomi's surprise, her shock.

"Are you Mrs. El-Karif?" Nomi hears someone ask. She looks up and sees an attractive blond woman standing above her. It is unusual for someone to open the heavy iron gate, and walk up the stone path unheard. Nomi used to have a dog to keep the Arabs away, but he had run off and she had not gotten around to replacing him. She had to keep them tied up all the time, otherwise they ate the chickens.

"Who are you? Do I know you?" Nomi asks, not unkindly. "Would you like to buy my saluf? It's the best in Jerusalem."

"I am a friend of your nephew's. I love fresh breads, but I live alone. I can't take more than three or four."

Nomi smiles; she would have enough money for dinner for two today. New energy pulses through her fingers as she works, kneading and then rolling the dough paper-thin on the sun-warmed stone.

"I came to talk to you about Yoeli," Karina says softly, as she kneels down beside Nomi. "I know your boy. He's a wonderful blessing."

"You know my little Yoeli?"

"Yes. He helps me sometimes in my dance studio. He cleans up, gets food, makes coffee for the customers, and I pay him a little. He's a big help and he loves to watch the dancing. Hasn't he said anything to you?"

"No," Nomi answers. Her eyes never leave her work. She can feel her heart beating faster, although she does not know why. Her shoulders sag suddenly and she looks as though she were falling.

"Are you all right?" Karina asks, putting a hand gently on Nomi's shoulder. Then Karina lowers her voice. "I can feed your nephew for you, Mrs. El-Karif. I can make sure he goes to school and he will help me. He won't have to get up before the sun and walk around the market anymore and you will be able to rest, maybe even go out a little and get your life back, your health."

Nomi continues to knead dough; her lips do not move and her head is bent over her work.

"I have no husband, no children and he is good company for me. I don't live far away, the Russian Quarter. He can visit you often and you won't have to worry about feeding him any longer."

Tears rush to Nomi's eyes, but she keeps them focused on the warming pitas. If they are on the heat for even a minute too long, they will burn and end up useless, bitter, a waste of precious flour and spices. She would have to toss good food into the garbage bin. They would not be valuable any longer, not even as feed for the chickens. If the chickens don't reject them, the hilbeh will make them sick, it is better for them to eat hard, tiny stones.

"Clothing, everything, I can take care of everything. Like another aunt I will be to him. I'm too old to begin motherhood, but I could be a wonderful aunt, like you." Karina's singsong voice is low. "It must be terribly hard work to clean people's homes. When you need a rest from it and can't work, he is hungry and…"

Karina's voice trails off as she sees Nomi's tears landing on the hard, dry soil. She has turned her face away from the stranger.

*

"Anat can go live in that apartment anytime," Yoel continues, but his voice is weak. Still, it jars me. Wasn't he asleep only a moment ago?

I don't know if he wants Anat to stay. I pick a few stray blades of grass that are pushing up between the patio tiles, under the pergola. Yoel helped us paint it; showing up every morning for three days before breakfast with his black tool belt secured around his waist and a can of rust-colored varnish. He must have caught a 6:00 a.m. bus to arrive at that hour.

Suddenly the sky is the color of dirty bathwater; rain clouds are forming like long lines of children at recess.

"I will even pay the tenant to go if that is what she decides," Yoel adds.

He has ignored my silences. I know he needs to catch a bus home soon or he will be late for his shift. He used to drive a Harley-Davidson, like my father, but lately he's been bussing. He tells me he's too distracted to drive.

"It must be very hard for you," I offer. Finally. "To keep living there with tension."

"Last night she came home from work and told me I was nothing but a fag, just an old fag," he said, but with each word his voice shrank.

Anat knew Yoel was gay when they married.

"She has a boy's body," I overheard my mother say once on the telephone when I was still living at home. "Flat-chested, very straight, small, you know? He probably likes that about her. Do you know what it was like for him at work in the hospital before he married? The rumors had to stop as soon as he did."

I sped up the stairs into the protection of the bathroom, the only room with a lock, when I sensed my mother was aware of my presence. I imagined Yoel at work, carefully helping old men and women into their beds before he took their temperatures, and blood pressure. He had been a nurse since I had known him.

"She was pregnant with Liat when I married her, you know?" Yoel blurts out. I shook my head. Now it's dark outside. My son must have come home with his carpool and gone straight to the computer room. I visualize the apple cores spread around the keyboard, seeds fallen on the floor, they could choke the baby.

"Anat is staying for now, like your mother told you…"

My baby is crying. As I rise to go to her, I am distracted by other noises; the sounds of the heavy iron gate opening and closing, footsteps on stone and a bag dragging across pavement. The breeze was lovely now; all of the sweat had dried on the back of Nomi's neck.

"Doda," Yoel calls brightly, his thin schoolbag was covered in chalky white dust. When he sees Karina he stops short. He did not know that Karina had his address.

"Yoeli," Karina says, "I'm glad you're here. I want to talk to you and your aunt together."

Yoel focuses his large eyes on his aunt and her eyes meet his briefly. Then she is packing pitas carefully into a plastic bag. Yoel notices that she packs enough for two. He sits down silently on the ground between the two women. He is afraid if he opens his mouth he will cry.

The Wisdom We Already Know

City Center, Jerusalem, Israel

The zooming increases in volume with each second. *Vroom, vroom.*

Miri looks over her shoulder and screams. The motorcycle is aimed at Beni, still in uniform. Miri presses her back to the white stone wall and feels Beni's body against her own for the first time in two months. He covers her completely and she's frozen, barely breathing.

The motorcycle blasts over the spot where Beni had stood only seconds before, bashes into and over the curb, tipping onto the narrow Jerusalem sidewalk. The coldness of the stone presses into her back and the night is still; the popular cafes and bars closed more than an hour ago. Miri waits for her heart to return to its regular rhythm before she opens her eyes.

They had been on a quiet evening stroll, a reunion, and Miri had only stepped an arm's length ahead. Now, Beni aims his rifle at the motorcycle driver's temple, his face turned to marble.

"Friend! Friend!" begs the driver, in Arabic-accented Hebrew. He's wearing a white T-shirt and jeans. His hands are open and up beside his ears and he licks his lower lip.

Miri smells gasoline, sweat, terror.

"Friend, it was an accident," the driver begs, his hands inching higher above his head, which Miri can only see in the shadow of a streetlamp flicking on and off, shooting up her anxiety.

"I'm not your friend," Beni growls, in a voice Miri doesn't recognize. "David!" he calls. His eyes remain on the driver's hands.

The pounding of footsteps on pavement. David and Lila spring out of the night like comic superheroes.

In an instant, David cocks his M16. Now four sets of eyes are trained on the driver.

"Why didn't you call me earlier?" David asks.

Miri hears the guilt in David's voice—in his desire to act like an ordinary twenty-year-old hanging out with his girlfriend on a Thursday night, he had strayed too far behind.

"It was an accident," the driver repeats. His Adam's apple bobs up and down. There are two rifles pointing at his brain. Miri's heart pounds.

"You tried to run us over," Beni insists. "Some accident."

Beni's words rumble in Miri's ears. The driver was clearly speeding in the dark, along a narrow road, not unlike so many roads in downtown Jerusalem; he lost control of the wheel and hit the sidewalk. Or is that her revision? She wills herself not to consider a motorcycle ramming. There have been five car rammings in the city today alone. Or is it three rammings and two stabbings? She peers as closely as she dares at the driver. He doesn't look as though he went for a ride in the night to see what it would take to make a street bleed. He just looks terrified. Her head feels heavy, as though her thoughts are filtered through wet paper towels.

"Let him go," Miri pleads.

"Why? He tried to kill us."

"It was an accident. Please, Beni."

Beni lowers his M16. Miri's eyes are still fixed on it. In their apartment she gives the weapon a wide birth—never turning her back to it, but retreating away from it face-forward, like a worshipper at the Wailing Wall.

The biker doesn't exhale until David steps back. Miri notices the driver's wrists shaking as he grasps the handles—once, twice, three times and then *roar*.

The four of them crowd onto the sidewalk, listening to the motorcycle whine grow fainter until they are alone again. Miri reaches for Beni's hand, but it's on his weapon. David remains ready to fire.

Instead of the starry sky and the open-air cafes she still sees the Arab driver, his heart beating in his throat, his hand reaching up to touch his forehead, relief passing over him as he felt its wholeness, his remaining hand so slippery he can't grip the handle, can't escape.

Brass Knuckles

The brass knuckles of the language? Will you never stop asking me questions about reality when I specifically signed up for the Fiction workshop?

My father's language in reality is Arabic, if you want to talk brass knuckles. Whenever my father was angry, not just exhausted or impatient, it was Arabic he used and when you translate it into English it is positively obscene.

It is all about sleeping with your mother, sister or aunt, using descriptions of private parts, male and female (kos-emek, kos-auchtek—I do not believe you can publish these words, but for me they are seared into my brain like the mathematical timetables). Or it is meaningless to us, plain silly, like "shoe of your father," na'al abuk, said with such ferocity that my father's shoes became like two live hand grenades in the front hall closet with the mirrored doors.

I would hear those two words, na'al abuk, even if I was two flights up, and my heart would pound in my ears and I knew that my father had crossed that line, that his anger was as unstoppable as death.

For I had seen his clenched fists go straight through the front door, the gaping holes in the walls from one well-aimed kick; it was not my imagination, it was reality and it made the hairs on my neck stand on end, and my mouth ran dry and I could no longer think of anything beyond saving my own skin. I would retreat into my bedroom and push and pull at my dresser until it sat in front of my bedroom door.

It was the heaviest piece of furniture in the room. He'd never laid a hand on me, not so much as a finger, but the threat of it and the image of the flaked, white plaster blown all over the stairs and sometimes the hallways was enough. There are some events that don't actually have to take place for the brain to make the body react like a victim.

But you want to hear about language. His language is the dialect of the blue collar Arabs who did not flee, did not have the money to flee (or were not slaughtered by Haj Amin al-Husseini, the Mufti of Jerusalem in the early 1930s) and later became the Palestinians. It is the language, too, of Arabs in Yemen, learned from his mother's breast, although she herself had never set foot outside of British-Occupied Palestine and later, Israel.

Language in my house in Ottawa was used as a weapon. My mother could not understand Hebrew, but we could. It was used as a way to possess the children—who really possessed them?

The one who could tell them secrets or mock the other without the victim understanding a word. It was at times a cruel weapon my father used against my mother; he would lower his voice when he did so, drawing attention. She'd stand a distance away and cry, "I know what you're saying, you know? You think I don't understand, but I do. You're talking about me. I'm not a dummy." Pause. "Yeah, right. Sure. You think I don't know."

This consistent reaction only granted my father a greater prize. A smile would appear on his face and he'd nod his head in his eagerness to win, to prove that of course, we all knew the truth: she did not have a clue what he was saying and yes, he was talking about her.

As we grew older (I can only speak for myself) I lost respect for this marital game. They were both diminished in my eyes, and I swore I'd never marry an Israeli, even an Ashkenazi one, it wouldn't be fair.

(I proved myself correct when I turned twenty and came to Israel and began to date Israelis. The innocent young men would say, common phrases, "*Mah yesh lach*? What's with you?" And I'd bristle. At the first utterance of an Arabic syllable, which is not uncommon among all Israelis, I was signaling the waitress, practically diving for the check. There was absolutely no way I was going to suffer the languages of my childhood in my adulthood.)

But you don't want childhood diversions professor, you want to dredge me back to Ottawa again, the Ottawa I fled. The Ottawa of the 1970s and 80s. My mother played a similar language game. She went out of her way to make sure my father had no time for proper English lessons. Discouraged them. It was not important, she could fill out all of the forms, comprehend the bills.

So what if Abba could speak Hebrew, Arabic and at least some Parsee? So what if he could sit and read Rashi with me and do the Torah homework with ease—where we lived, if you didn't speak English well, you might as well have been illiterate (unless you were French).

In those days Ottawa was a WASP town. You could count the non-white students in my high school on the finger of one hand. It was not the multi-cultural city you see today and the sea of head-covered Muslim women was a puddle. There was no ultra-Orthodox kollel, no rivers of Lebanese restaurants and hairdressers. Chinatown was two streets, perhaps, half a block longer than Little Italy.

This means it was unusual to hear English spoken with any sort of an accent unless it was French-Canadian, or maybe today they say Québécois. I haven't been there in so long, not even for a visit.

My father's impossible-to-place accent stood out in a way that was painful to me, especially if he answered the telephone. He found it difficult to wrap his tongue around the English names: Colleen, Avril, Diana May.

"Say again?" he'd utter into the receiver, a perfectly polite phrase in Hebrew. But the girl on the other end was anticipating something like my mother's homegrown "I beg your pardon?" or "Do you mind repeating that please? One moment while I get a pen." Naturally, I would cringe. He could not write the message down in English and he found memos like: *Tell her it's Diana May and I need her to bring in the props for drama class, for the radio play,* bewildering, untranslatable, so I just never got them.

At family dinners, Friday nights, Passover, Rosh Hashanah, my father was the monkey at the end of the table. The black, mute monkey. He always sat at the end (which in my Zaide's apartment was literally out the door).

We were such a large family and their apartment was so small that they had to open the front door and the person on the end in apartment #512 was eating their matzo balls and brisket with their elbows in the hallway and their backs in the corridor.

If my father's kippah fell off of his head, it was most likely to be trampled on by one of the curious Gentile neighbors, pretending to make yet another trip to the elevator. My father was likely to return home smelling of these hallway smokers who puffed vigorously, as the building was strict about entering the elevator with a lit cigarette in your hand. He came home with foreign smells, as befitting his foreignness, as though we had not eaten in the same room.

My big macher uncles barely grunted at my father and it always sickened me, the way my father would lower his head in a hello, keeping his eyes on the green carpet. I do not recall more than a Gut Shabbos exchange between my Zaide and my father, even if the evening lasted into the night and my Bubby was reluctantly grateful that my father was happiest washing up the dishes in their tiny kitchen or taking out the garbage. At least he was good for something.

At the Passover Seders my father never uttered a word from the Haggadah as his Sephardic Hebrew was an affront to my grandparents' Ashkenazi pronunciation of the Hebrew words and he would never read English publicly. He was simply skipped over, without ceremony, automatically, as one would push a button to begin a garbage incinerator.

He never said a word about it and we, the eight children, didn't either. What was there to say and to whom would we say it? We took it for granted, that's how it was. Still, my parents' marriage endured these language wars and that must count for something. Sometimes it even drew them closer together.

I will never forget one New Year's Eve. Not Rosh Hashanah, but December 31. One of my brothers worked in a prestigious government building (in shipping and receiving or it might have been in security at that time).

I worked there, too. It was a perfect job for a new university student: a coat check girl. All I had to do was wear black and white and smile for the first and last thirty minutes of any evening. The rest of the time I minded the coats and studied or researched my English essays.

They held the most expensive New Year's Eve party in town, with the top bands playing and an open bar at every turn. I always opted to work. I had no sentimentality toward this night and the pay was double.

Besides, I was bombarded with comments like, "Poor girl, she has to work on New Year's. Here's a big tip, sweetie." In short, I cleaned up, coming home with five times the pay of any other night of the year.

My brother invited my parents to the party. I don't know why. Neither of my parents drank, approved of drinking, endorsed smoking or enjoyed loud music. They looked down on it, something they shared. It was a goyshe thing to do: smoke, get drunk, it was for people with no class.

Right after midnight my parents had had enough and they headed down to the parking lot. But someone had blocked my father in. That someone was there, drunk, white, Canadian. My father asked politely. He said: "Won't you move your car? My wife and I would like to go home."

"Go back where you came from! You stupid Arab."

I saw my father clench and unclench his fists. He was dark; he had a black moustache and an accent. It was true; everyone thought he was an Arab, something I inherited, but in a less clear-cut way. I was accused of being everything from a Wop to a Leb and anything in-between. I recall (admittedly) to my satisfaction one night in a French bar:

"You are the most beautiful Iranian girl in this whole city. The most beautiful Iranian girl I've ever seen," said to me in a slurred Iranian accent, trying hard to sound Canadian. I could feel his breath on my face, smell the alcohol, see his brown fingers settling on my shoulder.

"Really?"

"Yeah." He inched closer. My back was up against a wall.

"It's just...that I'm not Iranian."

"You're not? Oh, come on now, beautiful. Don't you like me? I'm Iranian. You think I don't know Iranian girls? Come on, what are you then?"

"Well... I'm Israeli, actually."

If I had told him I had AIDS after we had just shared one glass, he could not have reacted any differently. He jumped back, his facial expression had transformed from one of lust to one of disgust. The ranting began: "How can I live with myself with what I am doing to the Palestinians? I'm a murderer, a Nazi. I should be put behind barbed wire." I guess beauty is only skin deep.

But we were with my parents in the underground parking lot, with the drunken man on New Year's Eve. I knew what was coming.

"Please move your car. We'd like to go home."

"Why don't you go back to your own fucking country? Why do you come here? Damned Arabs!"

"Are you going to move your car or not?"

"I'm not gonna move nothin'. What are you gonna do about it A-rab? You come near me and I'm gonna call the cops."

Pow!

The man was lying on the concrete, blood spurting from his nose. My pretty mother stood silently. My hand covered my mouth, but I said nothing. My father put his hand in the man's pocket and took out his car keys. On the ground, the man moaned, but did not open his eyes.

My father moved the stranger's car. He tossed the keys onto the man's chest. The entire time he muttered under his breath in Arabic, "Kos a-denic, kos-ememars." I knew I had to get back to the coat check. My mother and I remained silent and I watched my parents pull away, her head on his shoulder as he drove.

Arab-Israeli Assumptions

After class my new friend Valerie is nowhere to be seen. I remember she'd mumbled something about a research paper, but it's not clear to me what she was talking about. I'm too shy to ask anyone else on my program if they want to join me for lunch and I'm avoiding my roommates—the complaint letter about Farzeen, the Palestinian graduate student who shares my apartment, still burning a hole in my brain.

I head to one of the Haifa University cafeterias on my own. Today I'm happy that my uncle has invited me for the weekend and to celebrate I'm splurging on a store-bought lunch. I can only really afford a snack, but I'm calling it lunch. I'm self-conscious about eating on my own but force myself not to hide alone in my room with take-out. I don't have to push myself too hard; I'm avoiding my apartment.

The cafeteria closest to the dormitory is packed and noisy. Most of the students wear jeans as they do at my home university in Ottawa, but I can't help but notice how much older Israeli students are, how many are pregnant or walking around with babies, as well as backpacks slung over their bodies.

I remind myself that most are here after two or three years of military service and another year or two of travel and work, even after marriage. Every woman I see, who isn't sporting a baby, appears to be wearing full-make up, and my face feels naked in comparison. It had never occurred to me to put on lipstick for a university class let alone eye shadow, eye liner, and mascara. One of the lights in the corner keeps flickering on and off and I look away. It's probably buzzing as it dies out, but it's so noisy in here, it's impossible for me to isolate the sound.

I stand at the end of the line, considering the menu. It takes me a minute to realize that the woman with the long hair standing in front of me is Farzeen. Before I can stop myself, my fingers are on her shoulder. She turns to look at me. She has long, not quite black hair that reaches her waist, brown eyes, pale, pock-marked skin. She is plain-looking. She wears black pants and a long-sleeved eggplant colored shirt with a high neck.

"Want to have lunch together?"

Farzeen tosses her long hair with one hand and turns back around. I shrug. Her hair is so close to me, I can smell her floral scented hairspray. I inch back. I tried. I keep my eyes on the sticky floor. There are so many languages being spoken so rapidly around me, my head swims. The smell of fried food is the strongest smell in the room, but I can't identify it beyond that. Falafel? French fries?

I note the smell of coffee and melted cheese. This is a dairy cafeteria. Days of watching delivery men running up the stairs with extra large pizza boxes have done me in. I want melted cheese, but I know I'll settle for a warmed-up cheese Danish with a café au lait. Pizza is still out of my budget. I will wait until I can order a whole one and share it with Valerie. One slice would be a tease and it's too social.

Finally, it is my turn to pay. I've already chosen the largest Danish I could find in the row of desserts and received it heated, along with my coffee and cracked olives on the side. The change clinks on my tray. I turn left and right, weaving between people, seeking an empty table and finally find a two-seater in a far corner next to the only row of windows that are pulled open as far as they can go. Outside I can see the base of the Eshkol tower, the highest building on campus.

I want to wash my hands, but I'm worried someone will remove my tray, take over my table. I settle for wiping them very well with one napkin and holding my Danish with the other, so that my hands aren't actually touching my food. The first bite is sweet and cheesy. I should buy one as a present for Valerie.

Bang. A tray loaded with a large salad, large sandwich, large Coke and a healthy slice of chocolate cake lands on the table. I raise my eyes and Farzeen is arranging the strap of her briefcase around the back of the chair opposite me.

"There were no other seats," she says. I can't read her face and it's rude to stare too long. I force myself to look away from her.

"It's nice to have lunch with you," I answer. I sound too formal. I clear my throat.

Farzeen settles herself in her chair and immediately tends to her food. She pours a clear dressing all over her green salad and mixes it with her knife and fork. With her first bite a cherry tomato lands on her lap. She blushes and fumbles for a napkin on her tray, but there isn't one.

"No big deal," I say. I hand her a napkin. She wipes her pants.

"Thank you, Miriam," she says.

It's a good thing I grabbed such a large pile. She lets the tomato fall to the floor, and fails to pick it up, allowing it to roll toward the next table. I watch it come to a rest under her chair, but I don't say anything. She's still a little red and is obviously concentrating hard on the rest of her salad.

"I'm sorry about the other day," I begin. There's a stone in my throat as the image of Dalit's complaint letter comes to my mind and I hear Arslan, my Druze roommate: *Please sign. I can't live like this all year. Farzeen hates me, she hates Arabs who do the army. My father is a career soldier.*

We are six students to an apartment in the dormitory, two students to a bedroom. As far as the university is concerned, Farzeen and Arslan are both Arabs. They make no distinction between Palestinians and Druze students. There's a dull burning in my stomach. I tell myself I chose an old pastry.

Farzeen shrugs. She looks at me and offers a small smile.

"Are there only Jews in your classes?"

I hadn't thought about this. I am unused to organizing the people around me according to religion.

"I didn't ask."

"Can't you tell?"

"No. Not really. I didn't think of it."

"You should pay more attention to who you're with. This is the Middle East."

"I guess so." I play with my hair.

"Do you like the professors?"

"Yes. I find them very professional and warm."

"You sound surprised."

"I guess coming from a Canadian university, I didn't know what to expect."

"I understand. I wouldn't know what to expect if I studied in another country either." She smiles at me and I smile back.

"Of course, I'd be prepared," she adds.

"I asked around but couldn't find anyone who'd been to Haifa and I spent most of the summer working two jobs to pay for the trip."

"I worked all summer, too. Teaching Arabic to children with special needs, you know? Learning problems."

"That sounds way more interesting than waiting on tables."

We are both quiet for a few minutes, while we eat. My Danish is finished in a few bites and I sip my coffee and ignore the olives. Farzeen still has half a salad in front of her. She hasn't even begun the sandwich or the cake.

"You see that table over there?" Farzeen points with her chin, her fork full of cucumber in mid-air. "First years. I tutor all of them in Arabic in the evenings. Most of them came to me from their older sisters, who I also tutored. I don't take money."

I squirm in my seat. Had Farzeen seen me tear off the translator advertisement while I was waiting in line for the phone? Is she telling me a real Jew who cared about other Jews would help them with their homework for free? Or am I the most paranoid person in this cafeteria?

"It's great you have the time." I try to catch her eye, but she's examining the contents of her sandwich, adding more pepper to the bread from a take-away packet.

If she is so generous with her fellow students, maybe she could be reached, reasoned with; Arslan's position needs to be finessed to her, that's all. Is it really necessary to throw a person out of the room before we even attempt to speak to her rationally? Arslan is not responsible for her father's career choices. It should be easy enough to make that clear to Farzeen. Who am I kidding? Am I so arrogant that I don't think Arslan would have attempted to speak to her on her own? There's a larger principle at stake here, that's obvious. I've just never been tuned into it.

Out of the corner of my eye, I see a man coming toward us. He is wearing a plaid shirt and jeans, not unlike many of the other students, and his face is screwed up with anger. He notices that I've seen him and picks up speed. In ten seconds, both of his palms are flat on our table. Farzeen jerks her chair backward.

His mouth is open, but his voice is low, a hiss. He speaks without a pause in between but I don't understand Arabic. For a moment he is silent, eyeing me menacingly and then looks hard at Farzeen. He speaks again, even lower this time, and I resist the temptation to lean forward. Farzeen leans farther back, but her eyes don't move from his lips. His spit lands on the edge of Farzeen's chocolate cake. I don't know if she notices.

When he finally pauses for breath, Farzeen puts her hands on her hips and yells unapologetically. No one in the cafeteria so much as raises a head. It is so crowded and noisy, the yelling blends into the orchestra of high and low-pitched voices in Hebrew, Russian, English, French, and Arabic. I rest my chin in my hands, my elbows propped up on the table, only inches from this stranger's big, dark hands—the same color as my father's, but without his beautifully sculpted nails.

Now the man, angrier than ever, flails his hands around in the air, but Farzeen continues screaming in a stream of guttural tones. She doesn't flinch, though he is easily twice her size. They speak at the same time, in an odd sort of competition because she drowns him out hands down.

Finally, he glares at me, spins on his Nikes and stomps away, still muttering to himself and shaking his head. The heavy smell of tobacco mixed with cloves is left behind for a moment after he is gone. He must smoke a pipe.

Farzeen chuckles and then laughs. The clunky, silver necklace she wears rocks on her chest as her shoulders shake and her black mascara runs onto the backs of her hands, as she wipes her eyes. She brings her hands together in front of her.

"Do you know what he said? That man? That Arab?"

"No. What did he say? Who is he?"

"He's one of the student teachers in my history class. I just met him last week. He's new. He could use a good pinch." Farzeen stops speaking and I imagine her standing up and squeezing the angry man's skin between her fingers. I inch my chair backward. She picks up her Coke with both hands, drains the cup. I am afraid to speak; afraid she'll get distracted and stop explaining.

"He was very angry. He said we are traitors, shows-offs. He said who do we think we are?" She dabs at the corners of her eyes with a napkin and tosses the crumpled napkin over the chocolate cake. "He accuses us of being influenced living with Jews in the dorms."

"I don't get it."

"He said no one is fooled by us sitting here, pretending to be Jews, speaking in Hebrew. Anyone can see we are both Arab girls, so who do we think we are fooling with this fake Hebrew nonsense?" She throws her head back and laughs again and her hair sways over her chair.

My own hair is as black as Farzeen's and my skin is at least two shades darker than hers, which is merely sallow, mine is somewhere between toffee in the winter and bronze in the summer.

My mouth drops, but then I smile, too.

"I tried to explain to him that you are a tourist from Canada, but still a Jew and you want to practice your Hebrew, but he wouldn't hear of it. Arab girls from Canada don't come here he insisted. Selective hearing or what? Called me a show-off, a liar, and an embarrassment to my people. Oh well. We must have deserved an admonition, the both of us together. Would you like half of my sandwich? I don't have time to eat all of this now."

She picks up half of the sandwich with two hands and takes a bite. It looks as though she's eating some sort of white cheese with cucumbers and black olives on whole wheat pita.

"Here, you know what? I'll have them wrap it up for you. Put it in the fridge for later if you're not hungry now."

Before I can answer she is off to the cashier with the sandwich. In a minute she returns with the food wrapped in a paper bag, which she puts between us on the small table.

"That was really funny, no?"

I smile. At least we've shared a joke of some kind.

"I guess people make a lot of assumptions around here."

Farzeen looks at me. I can't read her eyes—again. At least she doesn't disagree out loud. She takes out her purse from her briefcase, unzips it and digs around inside. She reapplies her red lipstick and mascara with a small mirror and returns her cosmetics to her purse.

"I have to run."

She scoops up both of our trays, nods at me, dumps the remains in the bin and the empty trays on top of the garbage can. In a minute the crowd swallows her up. Out of the corner of my eye, I can still see the angry man. He waves a finger at me and clicks his tongue.

I imagine that man following me back to my dormitory and I really want to leave, but I have thirty minutes before my next class. I stand, and exit the cafeteria, taking the longest route, but the farthest away from the man who screamed at us.

It is only after I had opened the heavy cafeteria door, and walked out into the fresh air, that I remembered the half a sandwich Farzeen left for me on the cafeteria table.

Part Two: Marriage & Motherhood

The Wedding Day

The men are bearded and in black: pants, shoes, hats. Their shirts are Shabbat-white button-downs. Some of the hats are tilted, revealing a glimpse of the black, velvet *kippahs* underneath and patches of hair matted down with sweat.

The women are on the other side of the hall-length divider that is collapsible, on wheels and cold-coffee brown. It is easy to spot the married from the unmarried female guests. The married ones wear the requisite wigs that hang to the base of the neck, a few dare a shoulder-length look. Most are brunettes, but there is the occasional blond or auburn wig in the crowd. They have come by invitation of the groom.

The bride's small circle of guests is standing in the only available spaces the divider does not reach—mostly near the entrance. There men and women mingle, both dressed in pants. Except for the few who are staring at the "religious section," their backs are turned away from them, creating a second, human divider.

The hall displays neither color nor atmosphere. The chipped paint on the generic white walls and the hanging light bulbs do nothing to suggest a celebration. There are modest bunches of red roses on each of the fifty tables (twenty-five on either side of the divider), covered with sunset pink tablecloths and matching napkins. After surveying the hall, the groom was satisfied that no one could accuse him of worshipping the material world, and he immediately beckoned the manager to inquire about a suitable wedding date.

I try to concentrate on what it must look like outside: the rabbinic-looking men and the women in their full-length stockings, who seem to be either overfed or mannequin-like, nothing in-between—unless they are visibly pregnant. Trying to concentrate on an image is a calming technique I am using after seeing the rat that has just run between my legs, and under the toilet stall door.

The cubicle does not easily accommodate the toilet, me, and my female guard. The lack of space compounds the awkwardness of the situation. How can I use the toilet in these tight shoes, made of non-breathable fabric, this gown with the train that could match a tug-of-war rope for length, a wobbly veil that was fitted for my older sister's head, in the presence of an overdressed eighteen-year-old girl—flattened between the toilet roll holder and the jutting door lock—and the rat (rats?) that has just shot out, presumably from a crack in the wall behind the plumbing?

The rodent entangled itself briefly in the bottom folds of my pearl-white gown before it scrambled under the inch of space between the locked door and the faded, blue-tiled floor.

The teenaged girl, Yona, is my bodyguard for the day. Her straight, black hair resembles the wigs of the dozens of married women in the hall, and her smile is so wide it envelopes her ears. She is the daughter of my husband's new next door neighbor, soon to be my next door neighbor.

Dreams of marriage were never far from the young girl's mind, her mother had confided in me, and volunteering as a bride's bodyguard was supposed to bring her good luck. For Yona this meant her own wedding day, her mother stressed, in a way that let me know she shared her daughter's dreams.

The teenager is not a black belt on guard against potential lechers and thieves, but a guard against metaphysical dangers. She is supposed to act as a spiritual protector in order to thwart the evil eye and the evil inclination, and any other evils that might be floating around Jerusalem on this unusually sunny day in January.

The evil inclination—I had learned only a week ago from my bridal instructor, Fruma—takes countless guises and it is particularly jealous of young and fertile brides. Avoiding this threat required me to appoint a lookout, who would not let me out of her sight for the twenty-four hours before I became a married woman—not even to use the bathroom.

Fruma is one of the few streaked blond-wigged women outside. Two months ago, I could never have imagined her existence or the reality of any one of the Orthodox Jewish guests, now chirping and fluttering in the unmemorable hall in one of Jerusalem's religious neighborhoods.

How did I come to meet someone like Fruma, let alone employ her to teach me about the ways of Jewish marriages? This question crabbed its way into my brain, in spite of my efforts to suppress negative thoughts, which arguably is difficult to do between the sounds of toilets flushing in the stalls on either side of me. The rat must be hiding, I reasoned, or someone would have screamed.

I admit that Fruma's explanation about the guard did not take me by surprise—not after I'd spent twelve consecutive Wednesday nights listening to her instructions regarding the marital laws.

When she arrived at chapter three, which was titled, "Niddah" in the book, she re-titled the chapter "The Time When a Woman Needs Her Space." She began this section with the no's: no passing—not a baby, not a pen—no eating off of the same plate, no sharing the same chair or couch, no flirting, no, no, no. I remember her reacting to my amazed facial expression—was she putting me on? I was closer to thirty than twenty, and I did not regard myself as a gullible girl.

"Are you telling me that I can't hand my husband a pencil when I have my period?" I interrupted her to ask.

Fruma laughed at my question instead of responding. It was a maternal laugh and she accompanied it with a hand on my knee, followed by a light squeeze, which almost caused the toddler she had sitting on one side of her lap every lesson to simultaneously lose his balance, and the pacifier lodged in his mouth.

Now she switched from the no's to the cant's in the same cheerful voice she'd used the first time she'd extended her warm, soft hand, after I'd knocked on her door for the introductory class.

"He can't make your bed, he can't eat your leftovers, he can't see any part of your body that is normally covered, he can't —"

I interrupted her again and asked if this was some kind of medieval joke. The smile reappeared and she touched my arm this time and shook her head. All of her movements were gentle. Most of the hour she read or talked to me, her seventh baby, a girl, nursed at her breast on the other half of her lap.

"Don't worry, Miriam. You'll be pregnant or nursing most of the time. You'll probably be able to count the number of times you do this on one hand."

Pregnant or nursing? Neither of these words held any resonance for me. I had no younger siblings or cousins, and I had spent the better part of the last decade alternating my attendance between Ottawa's two universities.

I had begun undergraduate degrees four times. I'd majored in psychology and then history and then psychology again. I was determined to graduate in Israel after I was married. There did not seem to be any point in telling this to my new teacher. I was here because I had made a promise to my fiancé to be open-minded about the Orthodox Jewish lifestyle he had adopted.

As Fruma read on, it became harder to keep the doors of my mind unfastened, but I dutifully underlined the passages she stressed in my own copy of the book.

Fruma is a woman whose every second sentence seems to refer to God's will, who covers herself head to toe, with the exception of her face and the inch above her wrists, and who never exposes a single hair on her head. Yet, she did not hesitate when we got to chapter four. She called this section "What I was Allowed to do to Him and What he was Allowed to do to Me."

I tried to keep a straight face until the end of the chapter, knowing that the entire time she had one ear cocked, in case one of her five sleeping children—not including the two dozing on and off on her lap—might call out to her.

The former Bostoner's teaching voice was the same one she used to greet her husband—a rabbi who always came in halfway through the lesson. In the very tone with which she jumped up to say hello—somehow managing not to spill her children onto the floor, but to clasp them in her arms—and offer him dinner, she'd say things to me like: "I think a good tip is to put a towel underneath you."

What was I supposed to respond to that? "Oh. Well, thank you. I'll suggest that and see how it goes over, and it being Thursday, Good Shabbos Rebbetzin Shoemacher."

I'd dated my about-to-be husband for one year and we had just become engaged when he decided to lead an Orthodox Jewish lifestyle and suddenly refused to so much as hold my hand. Now—trapped by a rat in a bathroom stall—the doubts creep under my veil and around my hairline like head-lice. Had I made the right decision? I rest my forehead against my bare right hand and my focusing techniques are replaced by the images that brought me to the first time in my life I had a helper in the bathroom since nursery school.

My husband was graduating with a degree in law when we met and I was starting my undergraduate degree—again. Once we both realized that our relationship was serious, there was the usual heart-pounding romance, the love letters and poetry exchanges and then the debates about whether or not we should make our home in Israel. My sister, Lillian, a decade older than me, had written to me repeatedly over the years, asking me to join her on a kibbutz in the north of the country. We decided to have an engagement party in our hometown and the wedding in Jerusalem.

Finally, I was wearing an engagement ring that sparkled after I rubbed it with Colgate toothpaste, like the salesman had said, whispering the tip in my ear like a secret, free with every purchase. The modest invitation list followed—how many friends and relatives did two people from Ottawa have in Israel, or who could afford to pay for a trip to Jerusalem?

There were pauses afterward in the amount of time we spent together. At first, they were hardly noticeable, like the minutes that slip by between the salad and the soup, the soup and the chicken. They grew longer. Then there were no longer any words to interrupt the silences. Finally, I was alone with my sister—who had flown to Ottawa to celebrate my engagement—and the graphic artist. We were in an office that was small for a broom closet; I was under instructions from my fiancé not to use anyone "too caught up in the external world," and so I was using a freelancer.

I kept looking at my watch, at first casually and then in earnest, until my older sister just said it: "He's not coming to choose invitations, Miriam. Let's cancel the order before it's too late. She's an old friend of mine from high school. She'll understand." Then her arm around my heaving shoulders.

I was unprepared for my would-be husband's explanations. "I want a spiritual life. I want more. I want meaning. All kinds of smart women just like you become...." But there was no hiding the betrayal. "How long have you been planning—? Meeting with Rabbi _? When were you going to tell...? I planned a move all the way to Israel for..."

A month later the plane left for Israel without me.

There was not a day when I did not download an e-mail, answer a phone call, read a fax. "Please. Miriam. Just listen." After six months I forgave him long distance. Okay, so I wouldn't drive on Saturdays—who's brave enough to drive in Israel any day of the week? I flew to Jerusalem with my wedding dress and a fax with Fruma's address in my suitcase.

The guests my husband invited to the wedding are his new friends and he wants to share them with me. I rub my temples, trying to clear my head, but not for long; I need my hands to steady myself against the appearance of the second rat. This time Yona shrieks.

My helper is supposed to be holding up the train of my dress, so that it does not get soiled, but now that she's screaming, she forgets her role. I reach up to comfort her and blush at the ridiculousness of the situation. I am sitting on a toilet with my new underwear around my ankles, reaching up to comfort a frightened girl, turned guard in a bathroom stall, who is trying not to step on my wedding gown, my feet, and a rat. Someone is knocking on the door of the stall. I hear a voice that I cannot place: "How is everything going in there?"

I want to transform into an inclination, evil or otherwise and disperse, like toilet spray, into the air. I imagine the woman behind the door is thinking it is a good deed to make the bride happy—surely, she sees the train of my gown trailing under the door—and hoping that a kind gesture will encourage temporary blindness to the bride, whenever a rat scuttles by.

I have been a married woman for an hour and I am already taking on a maternal role. I pat Yona's arm and mumble something about "being just fine" to the door. Then I go on about how they're more afraid of us than we are of them. It seems to work and Yona apologizes and falls silent, but her eyes keep darting to the hole behind the toilet.

Twenty-four hours have passed since I have been allowed to eat or drink—with the exception of a glass of water that I poured down my throat in the *yichud* room, where the new couple is directed after the wedding ceremony. They explained that a wedding day should be like Yom Kippur. Now I cannot remember who "they" are. Was it Fruma's husband, or Fruma herself, or was it my new husband who told me this? My memory seems to have splintered along with the simple glass Kiddush cup that broke around my feet under the bridal canopy.

The cup was shattered shortly after the groom took the thin gold-colored band, we had precisely fitted for my wedding finger, and slid it down my pointer finger with such force that my eyes widened and I sucked in my breath from the unexpected pain. This preoccupied most of my time in the *yichud* room—trying to wrench the plain ring back up and off of my finger, while I berated my new husband.

"Are you crazy? If you have to force something so hard, doesn't that tell you anything? Like maybe it's the wrong finger?"

And he, tripping and stumbling, visibly trembling, his thin hands gliding above the surface of my shoulders in a pseudo-touch.

"I'm so sorry. I'm so sorry. Did I really hurt you? Let me see. Come closer. Did I tell you how beautiful you look? Did I tell you how happy I am? Oh, I didn't know. I'm sorry."

It was done. There was no point in answering. Besides, I was busy sizing up the window. Would I fit? Perhaps if I took off this gown, I might make it through. But did I bring a change of clothing? The fear of being in the center of attention that had gripped me since childhood quickly became a force greater than the pain in my finger.

While I was pondering possible escape routes, the clamor from outside grew like greedy flames. "*Kesad merakdim lefnai haKallah?* How do we dance before the bride?" I shrank. This was the first Jewish Orthodox wedding I had ever attended and the horrors kept coming. Wasn't the fiasco about my dress enough? I hear Fruma's well-meaning whispers over the remarks of the women washing their hands and the sounds of their chatter as they reapply make up in the bathroom mirrors—was it only an hour ago?

"The rabbi thinks your dress is a little too umm low in the front. He won't marry you this way."

"What? I haven't seen any rabbi. How can any of those men see me over this divider?"

"Yes. You're right. Silly me. The rabbi hasn't seen you, of course. You're right," she said again, revealing her nervousness.

"It's really umm his rebbetzin. She doesn't know you and she...well...how about putting a tablecloth around you?

Just for the ceremony. It's white. It'll blend and you're so gorgeous."

"What? Am I hearing right? You want me to get married in a tablecloth? This dress cost a fortune. I had the seamstress lengthen the sleeves especially to be considerate. It cost extra."

"I know, Miriam. It's my fault. I should have asked you to show me the dress before."

"You can't see a thing. This dress is beautiful."

"I know. It's the scoop neck. It's just...they prefer high collars, you know? To the neck. I should have told you. Let me put this tablecloth around your shoulders. Who is going to see?"

"You want me to get married in a tablecloth? Are you for real? You want me to walk up the stairs and outside in front of all of these people with a tablecloth around me?"

The reality of what Fruma was saying was enveloping me slowly, sinking in like animal teeth into a bone. Fruma must have sent the caterer or someone else over to distract my mother because my eyes searched for her without success.

"Come on, Miriam. You don't want to make a scene. Everyone is starting to wonder about the delay. We'll wrap it so it looks like something else. What's important is you're getting married, no? And to a mensch who adores you."

"You're serious. Listen, this is too much. Sorry. I can't do this."

"What if the rebbetzin slips out and finds you something nice to cover you up?"

"Cover me up? I should just walk out of here. There's nothing wrong with my dress. There must be dozens of rabbis in this room. I'll ask someone else. I don't care. "

Silent tears were running down my face. I knew only seconds separated me from a crowd of women who would all want to know why the bride's mascara was running. I tried to dart over to the bathroom—but how does a bride not attract attention at her wedding reception? Then the salt arrived to turn my fresh wound into a scar; my sister's eyes had never left me and neither had her ears, she made a beeline for the bathroom, the same one I was in now.

"You see? I told you," she began at full throttle. "You are so naive. I'm not mom. I'm not just going to nod and smile, like a dummy. You know nothing about religious life in Israel. Listen little sister, I'm ten years older than you. I know a few things. I've held my tongue long enough. I had a close friend on the kibbutz who made the same mistake you're about to make, and after ten years I watched her set her wig on fire. She bussed back to the kibbutz, sat in the soccer field and burned it. Is this what you want? It only gets worse, let me tell you. You don't know what these people are like. I've lived here for years. Miri, you're about to ruin your life. You see! You see! Look what they've done to you already and you're not even married yet."

"Come on, Lillian." My mother's voice. Neither of us had heard her come in.

"This isn't helping. Leave her alone. You just leave her alone. He's a nice boy. He loves her. Who cares about the rest? That lady, rabbi's wife, whatever, she's gone to get you something nice. She'll be right back. No one knows anything. Go on, Lillian."

I wiped my tears and looked at both of them without speaking. I left them there at the sink, Lillian's face tangled with anger. The image of a faceless woman striking a match with one hand and holding a head of brown synthetic hair in a grassy field with the other alternating in my food-deprived mind with the image of myself in an airplane, waving goodbye to my fiancé, his body shrinking on the runway below.

I have stage fright and I no longer need to use the bathroom.

"I think I'm done, Yona. Can you hold the ends a little higher, so that I can get up?"

"Of course."

I try to pull up first my underwear, and then my pantyhose, and Yona tries not to see me. She busies herself with the door lock.

"You don't have to worry. I won't say anything about the rats to the other guests. I hope there's none in the kitchen. Ha, ha," she says to me, on our way out.

I believe this is Yona's way of telling me that she isn't going to eat a bite and she has already prepared some cover-up excuse for when the others sitting at her table—who might not have witnessed any four-legged creatures in the bathroom—ask her why the food on her plate remains untouched. I nod at Yona and feel unsteady; I am still light-headed from the fast.

My eyes search for my husband. Moments ago, in the yichud room, he had laughed when I mentioned to him about escaping through the window. He insisted that this was foolishness, that the crowd was waiting for me and I owed it to them to appear. I had gulped down a glass of water from the tray of beverages and told him that I needed to use the bathroom. Luckily, Yona was still on guard duty and she was the first person I saw when the door opened, seemingly by itself. She managed to steer me to the ladies' room, even as the sounds of clapping hands and stomping feet grew to a roar.

Now my groom sits at the head table—beaming. Around the chair at his side is the luxurious rabbit fur shawl the rebbetzin had left the wedding hall to borrow for me. It fit perfectly and complemented my gown. Anyone would have thought I had planned to wear it; it was a winter wedding and the canopy was outside, after sundown. Why shouldn't the bride have an eye-catching stole to ward off the Holy City's evening chill?

I read my husband's medium brown eyes: Would I forgive his choice of rabbi (He had only known him for a month and selected him on the recommendation of a friend); the rebbetzin (She didn't mean harm); the stole (It was lovely in the end, wasn't it? Didn't a thousand complements rain down like manna when I wore it?); the bruised finger? (It didn't still hurt, did it?).

My flower-covered chair is pulled back. My sister's place is empty. In the background the singing begins again "Kesad merakdim lefnei haKallah?" The band starts playing. The dance floor fills and I watch as my mother leaves the head table, hands extended, head held high. Now she is part of the circle of dancing women. Then Fruma and Yona each take one of my mother's hands and form a new circle in the spotlight.

With my hand cupped to my husband's ear, I whisper, "Did you know there are rats in the bathroom?"

Roller Coaster

Miriam was too late getting down the stairs. By the time she made it into the living room it was over. She could only look from her son to her husband. Shock parachuted into the room like an invisible enemy.

That's not completely true. The whole truth hurts Miriam's stomach and she skips over it in the retelling, even to herself; the shame is too great. The truth is she had made it into the living room to witness her husband Beni enraged. His hand clutched her son's iPod high in the air.

Smash! The first hit divided the iPod in two. Beni bent down, snatched the largest piece and hurled it to the floor, where it broke into still more pieces. He repeated the action of seeking out the largest piece and destroying it until there was nothing left, but tooth-sized plastic bits. Miriam brought her hands to her cheeks, but sound was trapped in her throat.

She knew that she should never have left the two of them alone, not even for a breath, not even because they had five children all younger than eleven who needed her, too. It wasn't enough of an excuse. When would she learn?

In the morning the family had decided on an outing to SuperLand, an amusement park in Rishon LeZion. The schools were closed for the Hanukkah holidays and it was common for parents to take off work, too. Family time. They had to leave early if they were going to make it back for sunset, the optimal time for lighting Hanukkah candles. The earlier candles are lit after sunset, the more time left for passers-by to be reminded of light that can spring out of the darkness at any moment.

It still astounds Miriam how her mind surrounds the memory of that night with minute details: the warm, sunny winter weather; the crawling traffic on their way home; how she'd returned from candle-lighting on their front lawn to find that the dog had leaped onto the table and eaten the dinner they'd agonized over for an hour, before finally agreeing on a menu.

"What happened?" Miriam finally coughed out two words.

"Your fourteen-year-old got in line for the roller coaster and started talking to some secular girl in a mini skirt. They exchanged phone numbers and already became friends on Facebook. Is this why we take him on family outings? To meet *pritzus*? He broke the family rule. We do not start up with girls and certainly not ones from who knows where. She could be from any kind of home and he invites it into ours. For all we know she's one of those nutcases we read about who get boys to befriend her on the Internet and then meets them somewhere and has them kidnapped or killed."

"She talked to me. I didn't talk to her. There's no law against talking to girls. So, she's not religious, so what? She's not some stupid spy. Dad is nuts. Crazy. I can be friends on Facebook with anyone I want. And what do girls have to do with breaking my things? That iPod was a present for my bar mitzvah. You didn't buy it. I had all of my personal things on there. My pictures. My memories. He just grabbed it out of my hand. And if I smashed *his* iPhone, he'd freak out. I'm never speaking to him again! I hate him."

But Miriam only heard her son's voice after all of the menorahs were packed away next to the dreidels and leftover candles. After she'd finally dialed the right number and found him at a friend's. She had tried to turn her words into a soothing plaster, "Come home."

The silence that filled the house after their son disappeared broke only after three long family days with the children, nutritious homemade vegetable soups for dinner to balance out the fried potato pancakes and chocolate coin-shaped candies. After sunset Miriam did not look at Beni, neither during the candle-lighting, nor over the recitation of the Hebrew blessings.

While her children sang holiday songs with her husband and spun their dreidels for marshmallows, Miriam watched the light flicker in the window pane. She tried to accept that she was a mother who did not know where her son was and had not known for a while, but it was like trying to accept an incoming missile. She blinded herself to her son's smaller menorah that sat unlit in the window, cold and uncared for.

They lit one large family menorah together, but Jewish boys over the age of thirteen were considered adults, and last year Beni had proudly purchased a second one in gleaming silver, which he insisted now on leaving unused in the window until the last day of the holiday was over, as though the candelabrum could reach out its eight arms and gather their son home.

In the dark, when the glow from the candles had long faded and the house slept, Miriam reviewed the scene. There had been nothing in the agonizingly slow car ride back from Rishon LeZion to Jerusalem to indicate what was coming— no narrow looks or change in atmosphere. Still, she berated herself for not sensing something in her husband's body language. If she had, maybe her son wouldn't have slipped through her fingers like the last moments of a dream.

After their son's departure, Beni had eyed her with fury, as though *she* had picked up a teenaged girl in a low cut top and mini skirt in Rishon LeZion's only amusement park. She knew he was waiting for her to assert he had done the right thing, that they couldn't allow their son to pick up loose girls in front of their very eyes, to expose this immodesty to his little sisters. But she couldn't black out her husband's arm, cutting through the air with all of his might and, in mental replay, she heard her son's cry as his iPod burst open on the tiled floor. She absorbed Beni's fury into her heart, where it began to dig a hole, and said nothing.

Miriam counted her blessings: Beni had swept up the pieces of their son's prized possession, sparing her at least that. Not one of her children had heard what was going on downstairs in the living room, or the front door slamming hard enough to sway the flames that were burning inside the glass box they used to surround the menorah, to keep it safe from extinguishing too early on the front lawn.

For the rest of the holiday, Miriam and Beni spent every moment with their younger children, answering their whims for ice cream, for another outing, for just one more video before bed. Their son's cell phone might as well have been smashed to pieces, too.

On the eighth night, Miriam's breathing changed rhythm when Elazar answered.

"I'm not speaking to dad until he buys me a new iPod."

"I'm not buying him anything until the boy demonstrates that he understands why I broke it."

The angry words flap around her head whenever a friend or neighbor asks: How was your holiday? But she can't reveal them. They burn. So, she buries them inside of herself, in the hole next to Beni's fury, the way her son buries the digital photographs of the girl in the white mini skirt and low cut top behind a Facebook code he thinks she doesn't know.

Reverse

Elazar walked straight out of the heavy yeshivah doors without turning his head. Once he reached the sidewalk, he would be indistinguishable from the other males in the neighborhood, in his crisp, white button-down shirt, black pants, and black hat. The sidewalks teemed with men on their way to evening prayers. Elazar had already prayed. It was September, still warm enough to swim outdoors in Jerusalem. Tonight, was unusually hot; there was little chance of a reprieve from the weather before the fast of the Day of Atonement.

With each step, Elazar noticed a different girl, not much older than himself, praying or reciting psalms on a bench, a passer-by dropping coins into charity boxes appropriately placed in front of street musicians, or men debating the Talmud. He felt as though all of the inhabitants of Jerusalem were intent on rewinding the last year frame by frame, bent on examining each word and deed, like a king counting his gold.

Only a year ago he was a boy, boasting about how he was going to fast until noon. He remembered crowing that a sip of water would not pass between his lips until *Yizkor*, when only the orphaned were allowed to remain in synagogue. Those whose parents were still living waited outside and tried to avoid eye contact; gloating on a fast day was a risk.

This was Elazar's first year past his bar mitzvah. Tomorrow evening he'd have to go the full twenty-five hours without food or drink. He came to a clumsily constructed stall on the corner of C. Road and Rabbi Y. Street. The mixed male and female crowd spilled into the road, and Elazar could not resist the temptation to watch the atonement ritual. Even in the dim light, Elazar could make out yarmulke-wearing IDF soldiers with guns slung over their shoulders, off-duty bus drivers in their light blue Egged shirts, cigarettes perched in their mouths, Ethiopian mothers with babies on their backs in rainbow-colored pouches, and American seminary girls in their wrist-length shirts and washed-out denim skirts that hid their feet. For Elazar it was an assault of sound and color after weeks of sixteen-hour days of study, the necessary amount required before the holiest day of the year.

Two *chassidim* stood behind the counter, but there was no other discernable order. Ten sometimes fifteen Jews were performing the ancient penitence ritual at the same time, each in his own accented Hebrew. Elazar thought it was a miracle the chickens didn't clash in mid-air as the atoners whirled them clockwise over their heads. The noise coming from the crowd and the clucking of the chickens gave Elazar energy.

Squawk! Squawk!

"I sinned, forgive me. May all of my sins pass into this chicken and it shall die instead of me...."

The chant that only last year resembled an old popular nursery rhyme was at once familiar and terrifying to him. He had not asked permission to leave the yeshivah.

Elazar watched the green twenty-shekel bills pile up on the makeshift cash register. This was the going rate for atonement in Israel's most sacred city.

Squawk!

"I've sinned. Forgive me. May all of my sins..."

Elazar's gaze was drawn to an older lady. She was standing so close to the chickens that she was practically on top of the black metal cages. Some of the others had already asked her to step back, to wait her turn, but she did not budge.

Suddenly, she was racing through the ritual, with a chicken spinning on top of her kerchief-covered head. Before the chicken landed back in its cage, the lady had turned around and began to run up the cobblestone, narrow sidewalk, as though a plague of locusts were after her.

"Wait! You can't steal the atonement. Twenty shekels, hey Grandmother, twenty shekels!" cried the two bearded chassidim. The chickens belonged to them. Elazar's mouth dropped as the two men abandoned their stall and ran after the elderly lady. He wondered if he had misjudged her age; his own grandmother had stopped leaving her apartment in the end.

The teenager sprinted after the two panting chassids. Elazar was worried that the narrow sidewalk was so full of pedestrians, he'd be pushed into the traffic by passers-by, or perhaps by an angel, sent to defend penniless atoners. The local taxis and buses that possessed the roads felt dangerously close. He decided that he had to find out what the two men would do to her on such a holy night and pressed on. When he caught up to them, the chassids had cornered the lady against a stone wall, although they remained at arm's length.

"Pay!" the chassids demanded.

"I don't have money," she responded.

It was impossible for Elazar to tell if this was true. The elderly lady looked like any religious woman in Jerusalem; mid-calf length navy blue skirt, and matching crew cut top with several chains around her neck of varying lengths.

"Borrow, we'll wait."

The old lady's head shook from side to side. She wiped the sweat from her upper lip with a floral handkerchief that matched her head covering.

"I don't have any money," she repeated.

"Go ask a friend or a neighbor to lend you some then."

"I don't have any friends or neighbors," she said.

Elazar saw that there were chicken feathers stuck to the bottoms of her running shoes. He hadn't noticed her running shoes before. Doubt crabbed across his mind. Perhaps, it was the chassids who needed an angel to protect them against an evil incarnation. Had she planned to run? He had never seen his own grandmother in sneakers. She only wore shapeless, black slippers, except for the Sabbath and holidays when she wore shapeless black, short pumps. It hurt to think of his grandmother. This would be the first year his father would be staying in synagogue for Yizkor.

"Last chance, Granny. Pay up." The lady shook her head again.

Squawk! the chicken complained.

"Well then," snarled the chassid. "This chicken is reversing! May all of the sins of this chicken go onto you and you shall go to your death instead of..."

Elazar's eyes widened as the chicken spiraled, counterclockwise high in the air. He froze.

"No! No, please! Wait!" the Grandmother screamed.

Squawk!

"...this chicken," the chassid intoned.

The teenager dug through his jacket pockets. He thought about the evil inclination disguised as doubt. He never used money at school. He knew he had none.

Before Elazar could check the pockets of his pants, the elderly lady had reversed again and sprinted across the street, disappearing, phantomlike into the first diminutive house.

The chicken hung upside down in the night air, its legs in the grip of the chassid. From Elazar's point of view the bird appeared to have only one eye. Now it blinked at the pavement, its beak opening and closing.

The chassids nodded to each other as they pocketed the twenty-shekel bill they'd received from the elderly lady's veined, trembling hands. Elazar watched the grandmother cross the street for the second time. He wished that she would break into a run, her blush so red that she'd glow, a warning in the Old City night. But she walked, like all of the woman he had ever known walk after synagogue on a Friday night, nodding and wishing each other, '*Gut Shabbos*,' as though she'd already been judged favorably.

Then Elazar remembered his own transgression and began to walk and then to run back to his yeshivah.

Different Rank

I see my father writing, bent over the kitchen table in Ottawa. The table is so large, there is no room for the six matching chairs; two are crammed into the double-car garage. The two cars are parked in the driveway.

The radio is on AM and my father pauses often to listen. He wants to hear his favorite on-air talk show host; the one who criticizes Canadian government policies; federal, provincial, regional, municipal.

I cannot imagine a place more governed than Ottawa. People phone in and natter about getting ripped off by dinosaur bureaucrats, who have discarded their human hearts in scrap-heaps, their compassion with adolescence. The host digests and regurgitates their anger. Next to Sunday morning evangelical Christian programming and *Divorce Court*, this is my Israeli father's favorite show.

Although I imagine a light snow dusts the driveway on this ordinary winter morning, my father is shirtless and his tan shorts reach his hairy knees. At seventy the curling hairs on his chest are gray.

The button-down, short-sleeved shirt he dressed in at dawn hangs over the back of a kitchen chair. The shirt is Chinese lantern red and it glows beside the dullness of the chair upholstery.

My mother has never chosen a stick of furniture that is not drained of color. On my father's feet are brown, leather sandals, they catch the sunlight from the oversized kitchen window. I cannot remember a morning when I did not see him with a rag, polishing each shoe in the front hall closet. His wide back is like his shoulders; both are clammy from his hour-long workout with the barbells in the basement, which he began after a thirty-minute jog, just as the sun woke up the winter sky.

My father is writing his memoirs in Hebrew for me, his only biological daughter. As I receive them in the mail in

Israel, I translate them into English and save them on my computer.

A computer is not something my father would approach; he is convinced that the microwave will explode if he pushes the wrong button. He prefers to wait for my mother to come home from grocery shopping or a Mahjong game with her girlfriends, or eat cold food, rather than risk a repair bill.

Sometimes I have to pick up the phone and clarify something with my father's adopted brother, Adi. "What was the name of the grass you boiled to eat?" but for the most part, I translate the letters on my own.

My uncle lives near me in Tel Aviv and he knows that I am translating his adopted older brother's letters. He answers my questions half-heartedly. There are many I-don't-remembers and who knows? but he is all I have. I have not met any of my father's other relatives in Israel, despite the fact that both of his parents, my grandparents, grew up here, and after a decade in Israel, I do not believe I will.

My two half-sisters are my father's stepdaughters. Their own father goes unmentioned in my parents' home, like a ghost that might be invoked by the uttering of his own name. It is as though each of them harbors the same fear; if they say his name, he will materialize.

Better to leave him as a fantastical figure. His interest to me growing up was limited; my parents were married to each other. What use does a girl have for what came before she existed?

I know when someone asks my father how many children he has, he answers "Two." This happens in stores and malls, sometimes gas stations or anywhere that a line forms. I have not asked my brother, Our-Stanley, if my father subtracts his two stepdaughters when they are alone together. I don't want to know.

My father is the type who jokes with salespeople, waitresses, security guards. He'll joke with them about taxes (*On the side, they all take cash*) or about marriage (*How are you*

Mr. Karif? Oh, I'm still married. Don't tell my wife.) and when I come into view, a young restaurant hostess or cashier might ask "How many others do you have at home?" There's a pause, the air thickens so my father has to inhale, like just before he bench-presses his daily 150 pounds and then— "two." He says it looking straight into his questioner's eyes and holding up two fingers, in a victory sign. I look the other way and neutralize my facial expression. What would mom say?

There is a block between me and my half-sisters. We do not exchange confidences along with our cast-off clothing and make up. Neither do we smear ripe green avocado on each other's cheeks, noses and foreheads to give ourselves, clearer, smoother, healthier complexions. No one will spy us giggling as we insert pieces of white ripped cotton between our freshly painted toenails (blue or red); chatting as we rub peroxide and lemon juice in each other's hair to create alluring highlights.

My sisters are three and four years older than me and they are best friends and share their father's looks between them (So my mother tells me. On the rare occasions when she is forced to talk about her first husband, I glean bits of information and save them in my mind like war rations). The features that resemble their father's the most have been divided up like an extra airplane meal: the older has his nose, eyes and hair; the younger has his mouth, complexion and frame. Neither of them shares our mother's beauty; it is Our-Stanley who looks like our mother: white, Ashkenazi, European Jewish face, sculpted like an artist's vision.

"Your mother makes girls look like boys and boys look like girls," I can hear my father telling me. "Except you," he'll add, after a pause.

I am not certain I believe his clarification. I know he is referring to Our-Stanley's smooth, hairless skin, thick, shiny hair, and fine features. My sisters spend a lot of time comparing the latest methods of hair removal and lamenting their blotchy cheeks and foreheads. I have my father's dark,

Yemenite-Jew looks. Only when I smile can you see the shadow of my brother in me. But it is the facial expression that has been carved between us; not the face.

If I had a nickel (I imagine the silver Canadian one with the beaver) for every time someone in Ottawa (at bus stops, in restaurants, in movie theater lobbies, between Carleton University lectures) asked me if I were Greek, Italian, or Portuguese, while I was growing up, I could buy a new uniform for every Israeli soldier.

I picture my father finishing his entry, looking for an envelope in the kitchen drawer, crowded with restaurant take-away menus and unopened bills. He does not reread what he writes.

Nothing is edited, deleted or added and every page is written to the bottom, with just enough space for a sign-off: *Love Abba*. Nothing more. Our-Stanley never asks my father to write anything except checks. At thirty, he has no bank account or car insurance and my mother still rushes to pour him chilled grape juice or chocolate milk, and to boil his dinner.

But I'm after something else: my parents' memories. As I try to raise my own children, I find myself wanting to know more about my own parents, their pasts and disappointments.

They have decided to give them to me, what they will allow themselves to recall. This could not have happened a few years ago. It would have seemed to them a silly request, a bad joke; a grown-up crying for a bedtime story and a nightlight. It is only now, in retirement, that they have agreed.

My father was home for a year, following my mother back and forth to the hairdresser, when he finally had so little to do that he sat straight-backed and covered white, lined paper from margin to margin for me. My mother told him to "stop being silly" and just write.

At a slower pace, she is doing the same. She is Ottawa born and bred; I don't need to translate her letters and she emails them. They do not arrive with love at the bottom of my mailbox like my father's letters.

My father's writing career is short-lived. By page thirty he is applying for a part-time job. Anything. He takes one at a non-kosher bakery, only a five-minute walk away from his home.

Now he is a seventy-year old baker. In addition, he makes change for the customers, packages their requests, but he remains the same appliance salesman he always was. He is still a man mocking the world, getting one up, and from now on I have to nag him for his letters.

"Abba, are you writing for me?" I ask him.

"Yeah, I will after. I'm tired now from work," he says to me. "Get this, Miriam."

I have called him long distance from Jerusalem. He does not believe in spending money on long distance phone calls, but in long hand-written letters. The kind I imagine people used to receive from a rider on horseback, minus the red wax seal.

Since his retirement he has loosened up; he allows me a brief long distance conversation if I phone him, before he insists on ending this outrageous use of good money and writing me a letter.

"There are French loaves and Italian loaves, right?"

I nod and I believe he can hear me nodding.

"The dough is the same. Exactly. One stripe for French, you know like a first sergeant and two for the Italian bread, like the one up. How do you say it in English?"

"I don't know. General? Colonel? I didn't do the army, Abba."

"Officer, I guess. It doesn't matter. Anyhow, that's the difference. A sergeant or a first officer, but they charge more for the Italian. Same dough, right out of the box. We just put the stripes and some oil to shine it and heat it up. Sometimes I work the counter and there's no more Italian bread. The people come and I say, 'Take the French, it's the same thing.' 'No,' they say shaking their heads like I'm trying to fool them. 'It's not the same thing; my family only likes the Italian. ' And I laugh and say, 'I make the bread, I'm telling you it's the same box; just the stripes are different, different rank.' 'No, I'll come back tomorrow.' And they walk away. First, they pay more and then they don't believe you. Do you believe these Canadians?"

To hear him talk I might think he had been in Canada for twenty-four hours instead of thirty-one years, that the government had interned him in a camp, like they did to the Japanese during the Second World War, instead of offering him full citizenship and complete benefits, after my grandfather smuggled his daughter's fiancé over the American border in the back of his green Ford.

Then my father laughs his huge laugh, like the ones the giants in bedtime stories laugh, before they gobble up their victims, or fall foolishly headfirst into bottomless pits or cauldrons of boiling water. His shoulders shake and his head tilts back and it is obvious he enjoys these public encounters.

"They pay more for stripes, Miri. This is people: stupid."

Did you finish the letter?" I ask, changing the subject.

"Yeah, I finished. Your mother sent it on the way to the hairdresser. If she didn't go, the Lebanese woman, she'd be out of business. Every woman in the shul goes to the Lebanese for the hair. You think she's laughing? I think this Lebanese is laughing all the way to the bank with the money."

"My hairdresser's Moroccan," I respond, trying to steer the conversation again. I know what he thinks of the money women spend on their hair and I have known it since I was in grade three.

"*Moroccai?* Yes, they all of them good with the hands. But she's Jewish, you're in Israel."

Telling me I'm in Israel reminds my father that the call is not local and he excuses himself and hangs up. I stand with the receiver in my hand, imagining him. I know he has stood up, rinsed his clear glass coffee cup out in the kitchen sink, without using dish soap and placed it upside down on the drying rack.

Dish soap is only for items my father considers dirty, not just used. I have never seen my father put a dish in the sink. If he spots a dirty dish, he aims himself at it like a jumbo jet coming in for landing.

Soon he'll be asleep. He naps every day since he has turned seventy. He'll lie with no coversheet, in his black boxer shorts, with a fan aimed at his muscular chest, and snore so loudly that my mother will flee two floors down, to the finished basement, if she hasn't gone out for coffee with a girlfriend. This is his life.

Abba

I was born in Jerusalem in Hadassah Hospital on Mount Scopus on the first of August 1936 to Yemenite parents. My father, Mordechai, was born in Yemen and came to Israel with his parents, who were very religious, like all of those who came from Yemen to Palestine. My mother, Nomi, was born in Jaffa-Tel Aviv, also to religious parents.

After I was in the hospital eight days, I had my circumcision and on the ninth day my father borrowed his friend's taxi in order to bring me home. This taxi was normally parked on Ben Yehudah Street in Jerusalem's downtown.

It was a fifteen-minute drive north to Mount Scopus. It was a Ford model 1932. My father drove it to the hospital and took us home to our Jerusalem Yemenite neighborhood. In those days we lived closest to Jews of the same background. Sephardic lived with Sephardic and Yemenite with Yemenite and so on.

Our house was large: three rooms plus a big garden, almost one dunam (a quarter of an acre) and it was surrounded by a tall fence, almost three meters in height. The law—a British law that goes back to 1920—was that all homes had to be constructed of Jerusalem stone, so the outside was the white Jerusalem stone you see today all over the city.

My parents bought the land before their wedding and had the home built in time for them to move in. It was the last house in the neighborhood, at the base of a hill. Before us, on another hill, was a large Arab neighborhood. Today the Israeli Supreme Court stands there.

We shared warm relations with the Arabs in the surrounding neighborhoods. They liked us because my mother honored them with strong, hot Turkish coffee, spiced with cardamom, or sweetened Nescafé. She combined coffees with her homemade cakes, offering a welcome break to the Arabs who always passed our home on their way to sell their fruits and vegetables each morning in Jerusalem's *Machane Yehudah* market. They never failed to give us fresh dates and *sabras*, prickly pears, in return. They picked them themselves at the break of dawn, when the dew was still fresh on the ground.

The way to our home was a series of unpaved dirt paths, all of which turned into puddles of water and thick clay-like mud in the rainy winter season. Our shoes were constantly dirty and wet, and in summer we used to fall on the uneven paths countless times a day.

I remember our knees were permanently wrapped in bandages from these nonstop falls. In the summer the view from our home was breathtaking; we were surrounded by wild flowers of every color; cyclamens of purple and red anemones filled the untended fields around us. The view was dazzling and the smell was powerful and fragrant, almost hypnotic. I am an old man of seventy and my Jerusalem is no longer, but I can still smell it.

Because we were the last home at the bottom of the valley, surrounded by hills, all of the water from Moadon Menorah and the surrounding area flowed downward, creating lakes of water around our home. When we walked home, we jumped from rock to rock in order not to sink into the mud or dirty our shoes. I always loved to look out the window toward the sky; the black clouds appeared to flow down from heaven, hiding the top of the mountain across from us in the valley.

My mother used to place bags and towels on the windowsills and underneath the doors in order to prevent the entry of the cold winds that blew into the house through the windows. In the middle of the room was a kerosene heater, called a primos. It was a feeble attempt to heat up the room. Later we bought an oven, but I was a soldier by then. The oven was more useful but, in any event, the house was always cold.

When I reached the age of three, my parents decided to put me in a nursery school, a *gan*. The one they chose was run by Rabbi Y. It was located on the way to Machane Yehudah, and it operated from 9 a.m. to 3:00 in the afternoon. This freed up my mother to work for the rich, Ashkenazi Jews in Rehavia. I stayed in the gan for a few weeks until my mother discovered that I had lice in my hair, and she took me out of the gan.

My new nursery school was called S., a half an hour's walk from my house. I stayed there all day, until 4:00 in the afternoon. The teacher was a *yekke*, German, who was very strict with us and whoever did not listen to her was punished.

We ate lunch there. It was vegetable soup that was tasteless with no flavor and no smell. Whoever did not eat it willingly had it forced into him. There were children like me, who were nauseated by the food and threw up. The teacher would take the vomit from the table and put it back on a spoon. Then she would feed it back to us while screaming "Open your mouth!"

For many of us, lunchtime was a cruel nightmare, but what could be done? The parents did not interfere, and they were happy that somebody was watching their children for the day. Her name was H.H. I never liked her, but there was nothing the children could do. She had a way of silencing a child: if the child cried, she would put a bandage over his mouth. If the children merely saw her with the bandage in her hand, they stopped crying immediately and choked on their tears.

In the afternoons, my mother would come to pick me up. I would come home, grab something to eat and run outside to play with all of the neighborhood children until darkness fell and I would hear the calls of the mothers, beckoning their children to come inside and go to sleep.

In the winters there were huge puddles of water full of frogs and they were a source of great amusement to me and my friends: to catch them. When we were frozen with cold, we would climb the wall of the bakery that was in the area, and warm ourselves by its oven. When we were hungry, we would cut leaves from the fields. We would suck the juice from the lettuce-like leaves. There were also flowers that we picked and sucked the nectar. We ate and enjoyed.

We had lots of mice and snakes in the house. There was a large ceramic bowl, full of *doora*, feed, for the chickens, and the mice would jump in and get stuck. They could not escape the smooth ceramic sides; they cannot climb.

So, the nursery school teacher would say "I will get them out." She would take a glove and catch them, and she would drown them in a bowl of water. A number of times a week she did this. What a job for a religious woman! When they finally left, my father rented the place to her sister, a hairdresser.

We had two rooms that my father rented out to the nursery school teacher and her family (the same one who made me eat my own vomit). Her husband had a shop on L. Street, and they had two girls.

The husband and wife loved the place because there was a big yard for their kids to play in. On top of the rent, my father had a good salary. The renters never liked us dark Jews, but the price was good for them. We had a chicken house filled with colorful chickens, goats, a dove house, and a big dog on a chain, who barked at anyone who approached. I was responsible for cleaning the chicken house daily and for cleaning the dog every afternoon. I would remove their waste and throw it on the ground behind the house, and there we would grow vegetables of all kinds.

My father checked daily after work to make sure I did my chores, and if they were incomplete, he screamed, and when he screamed, all of the neighbors would stick their heads out the windows. Later, when they met up with me, they would say "How does your father have the strength to scream like that?"

When he turned his screams to her, Mother would jump from the back window into the backyard and go to the neighbors, who pitied her. We never had a fridge; we bought her a box they called a fridge. Every time we heard a bell ring, we ran to the car and bought a quarter block of ice and put it in the box before it melted.

When we returned from school we used to down a bowl of vegetable soup with bread and *hilbeh* and rush outside to play until darkness fell. All week we waited for Friday night when we dressed in clean long pants, clean shirts, and polished shoes and ran to the shul to sing *Shir Hashirim*.

Until today I enjoy saying this in shul. In the G. shul in the N. neighborhood where my saba lived he earned prutot but had no doubts that God would help him make a living, and he taught me to give charity, a big mitzvah; even if you gave a pruta to the shul, it was something.

In my grandfather's shul, we took off our shoes. We walked on a clean carpet. I would sit beside my grandfather, open the siddur, prayer book, and shout *Adon olam* or *Shir Hashirim* or *Lecha dodi*. How lovely and what spiritual rest, *menucha nafshit*, just to run away from the house.

There was a pleasant smell in the shul from the old people's snuff. They would honor one another with the white or brown tobacco. Occasionally, they would give some to me, and they would enjoy it when I sneezed. In the shul we sat on straw mats and the rabbi would lead the prayers according to the Yemenite tradition. My mother always gave spices for *havdalah* and for Yom Kippur afternoons, a custom of Yemenites.

My father was an important man in the Labor Party, but I never saw him give his parents a *pruta*. They were very quiet and modest. My grandfather was the *shamash*, sexton of the shul, and also a ritual slaughterer (of chickens) and from this he made a living. Savta sold *hilbe* and *schug* and *saluf*, and even the very religious Ashkenazim came to buy from her because her food was so tasty, clean, and with plenty of aroma that gave you an appetite.

Binyamin was born when I was five years old. My father told me to come with him to Hadassah Hospital on Mount Scopus and we went with the taxi driver. He let me hoot the horn and I was thrilled. They put Binyamin in a wooden box they took from the fruit market, and after that he took my bed and we were four souls in one room.

My mother became ill and the doctor said she was working too hard and it was forbidden for her to get pregnant and to eat fried foods and fat. She said "My *menucha*, rest, will only be in *Gan Eden*, the Garden of Eden."

All of these illnesses drained her happiness and gave her endless stress. Her only enjoyment was her garden in which she grew spices for the shul for havdalah and all kinds of beautiful roses. Her secret was to take the leftover toilet water and use it as compost. It was excellent for the flowers and they grew beautifully, and on Fridays neighbors came and picked fresh roses for Shabbat.

One day in 1948, my father took me secretly behind the house and told me the fighters for the Jews would build an airport in the field across from our house. He said the army was going to build a shack with lights that would show the planes where to land and when to take off from the large field behind our home. The shack would be on our roof. For me this turned out to be an amazing experience, seeing the planes up close.

This was shortly after we received good tidings; all of the inhabitants of the Arab village, Sheikh Badr, across from the house had disappeared. We ascended the hill and walked from house to house; there was no one and everything remained. That's when the War of Independence, *Milchemet Hashichrur*, broke out.

One day workers came to us in the house and blocked the windows and the doors with sacks of sand. There was no water and no electricity, and Jerusalem was besieged. Food drop-offs were organized for Jerusalem, and the work to establish an airport began in a rush. Tractors flattened the ground, and I remember small airplanes landing for the first time, bringing supply-filled sacks to Jerusalem. There were always a number of soldiers on the roof. We built a little shack for them, and they covered it with wire for camouflage.

Mother reduced food and water consumption and later it was only for drinking. The soldiers liked her, and so they brought us breakfast from the military kitchen, and this helped fill our hungry stomachs.

Suddenly the Arabs began to bomb Jerusalem. The school was closed, and no one went to work. Everyone was conscripted into the military or to help in hospitals or to bury the dead. Across from the house, the dead were in crates one on top of the other. All day we heard the screams and the cries of parents and families who went behind the trucks. The situation worsened, and we received coupons for food and water.

I made a wagon with four wheels for olive picking in Emek Hamatsleva, the Valley of the Cross, and my mother also taught me to pick good plants to eat like *chubezah* and roots of various kinds.

We never complained, and in the night, my mother would wake me and we would watch the mortars flying through the sky. For her, this was an experience; she was very brave, unlike my father who was a coward. He went to work every day, even though the city was all but closed. More and more airplanes came every day. One time in the night, my mother woke me up to see a twin-engine airplane, a rarity. It brought food and cigarettes.

By some miracle, no mortar fell on our home or in our neighborhood. Perhaps we were too far from the Old City; the Arabs mostly bombed the city center. Every day we stood in line for our bucket of drinking water. We always stood quietly and patiently until the one in charge opened the lock and the cover of the water hole. There was a pail on a rope that we would throw into the water and fill up our bucket: life for the soul.

The days were hard—no food and little water and no radio to listen to the news. On the hill, across from the house, funerals took place all day. In daylight, there were the continuous sounds of the screaming and crying over the dead, and in the night, we would wake up to the shrieks from the mortars.

When the mortars were falling, we would flee to the bathtub; they told us that it was the most protected place because the bathroom had double walls. All of the windows and doors were covered in sacks of sand. On the streets, all was closed or broken; very few people moved around, mostly soldiers. There were military police searching for boys of conscription age who were hiding in houses and did not want to serve.

In the daytime, I went around the neighborhood with friends looking for food and collecting shells from bullets, just for keepsakes. My brothers were very little and did not understand what was going on; they only knew that when they heard the shrieks from the mortars, they needed to hide. Here and there, we looked at the small airplanes that landed and brought some sacks of food, weapons, and medicine to Jerusalem. All of this I endured while still under the age of thirteen.

When I reached the age of six, my grandparents decided to put me in a religious school called O. T. Most of the student population was from Rehavia, the prestigious and quiet neighborhood, populated almost exclusively by German Jews. The students were snobs and looked down on me. I was the only Yemenite boy in the class and stood out unbelievably. My first and second years as a student there were not bad because I had nice teachers and I got good report cards. They did not threaten or punish me, and I did not bother them; I was quiet and disciplined.

In grade three, it was another story. When I went out for recess in the large yard, I saw a group of children joined at the shoulders, their arms laced together like Sukkah decorations looped together to form a long line. They were singing gleefully:

To the Yemenites were born three boys.
One was fat and one was thin
and in the toilet the third fell in.

I was angry and hurt because I was the only Yemenite in the school. The teacher on duty looked at me and laughed, but it was not at all funny. I went into the classroom and sat alone. From then on, I hated the other students and the teacher, too. I thought about how I would get my revenge. I had German *yekkish* teachers, and my skin color bothered them. They would tease me endlessly, and they would pass by the rows of students and stop at me. They would look disapprovingly into my black eyes and twist my ears painfully. They enjoyed it, and the other children laughed. When I complained, they responded that I was wild and did not listen to them.

At the end of the year, I decided to leave this school, but my father refused to allow it. Every one of his answers was "No." I told him that I would leave and go to a school called B. Y. and register myself; I could not study, and I could not concentrate. Every day I went to school by force, with no desire, and, when the teacher passed by my chair, I would cover my ears and the teacher would see this and laugh and say "What a brave boy you are." I swore I would get my revenge on this teacher.

In 1954, when I entered the army, I was a driver for many officers who lived in Jerusalem. One day one of them said to me "Get the jeep ready, we are going to the Old City." I always had non-perishable foods in my jeep: meat, sardines, jam, and soups.

I gave as much of this as I could to my mother because my father always told me that he did not have money to buy food; he had to pay the mortgage. As a result, my mother had to clean homes of the Ashkenazim in Rehavia, and she cooked for them too. I knew my father was lying because the mortgage was already paid.

I entered the jeep, stopped to pick up my officer, and went to Jerusalem, arriving in the afternoon. My officer said to me "Take the jeep and have a good time, and tomorrow morning pick me up."

I thanked him and drove directly to the school O. T. I stood on the side and saw a Vespa, motor scooter, standing in the parking lot. I took off my paratrooper hat, put on a civilian shirt, and fetched a friend from the neighborhood, and he helped me put the Vespa on the jeep.

From there I drove to Lifta, a ravine at the entrance to Jerusalem, and threw the motor scooter down the ravine to hell until it reached the Cedron Valley and turned to rubble. I thought: This is what I do to *mamzer* teachers, who pull at my ears. I returned, and, at 2:00, I watched my former teacher looking for his Vespa. What a joy it was for me! The teacher walked home.

The next morning, I telephoned my old teacher at school. I asked him how he was, and the teacher asked who is speaking. I said "It is one of your students whose ears you used to pull for fun and enjoyment, and your Vespa I threw to Cedron in Lifta." My old teacher claimed to have no memory of such a student. I told him that ten years ago, I was the only Yemenite boy in his grade three class.

"Now for sure you recall me," I said, and then I laughed and swore at him and hung up the telephone. I went home to my mother and brought her food. She blessed me and I returned to the base.

I had an English teacher named P. who the class enjoyed because most of the students found it easy to learn English. They knew German and Yiddish, so they had a good basis for the language. He would point to the floor and say floor in English. This was his most common method of building vocabulary. I did not understand him, and there was no one to help me with my schoolwork at home. I failed English.

Next door to my home lived a smiley older lady, who gave private English lessons. She came to my house and asked me what the problem was. I must have told her about my troubles at school, or perhaps she overheard me complaining. She told me to come to her house once a week for lessons. I felt better, and I was not disappointed.

I had a gym teacher called K. from Russia. He only taught us baseball, and that was the one sport we already knew. We had a forty-five minute class, and, within that time, the teacher would line us up in a row and check our gym shoes to see if they were white.

Our shirts were also white and our shorts were blue and we had to write our names on every article of clothing. He never gave us exercises or allowed us to play soccer or games. Likely he did not know anything else, but he was the gym teacher. He was a good friend of my father's, and my father was very impressed with him.

With great difficulty, I finished grade three. At home there were problems; my parents yelled at each other and fought constantly. Because of their fighting I used to run away to my grandparents' home. They hugged and kissed me, and they knew why I had come. They used to make me little special *salufas*. I sat on the carpet and ate in peace and quiet, and I would help them bring water from the neighbors and my *savta* would bless me nonstop.

My grandparents lived in a basement without water or electricity. For light there were lanterns. There was always food, cleanliness, peace, and quiet. I never heard them argue. My *saba* took me to shul; I can still feel the warmth of his hand on my own. My grandfather used to kiss my hand and bless me: "*Yevarhecehah* Hashem *ve'ishmereha*," and he would put his hand on my head. In my grandfather's eyes, I saw only respect and beauty.

After I turned thirteen, I worked as a carpenter's apprentice for two years. The manager was Ashkenazi, a big *mamzer*, bastard, who always made sure that instead of learning carpentry, I would be a cleaner. I wanted to be a real apprentice. I repeatedly requested to be taught how to build furniture, but the carpenters never included me in carpentry work; I was like a foreign seed. I told my father that they were not teaching me anything and he would say it was not true, they told him they were.

Once I had a test from the government supervisor. He asked me to build a table. I did the best I could, and I got a mark of "not good." And he said, "What? After two years you don't know carpentry?" I said, "Tell the boss." Of course, this got me nowhere; the white Jews protected each other.

Finally, at sixteen, I demanded to learn and to stop being a cleaner. My boss responded that I would do as he says. I punched him in the face and he fell. I took off my apron and threw it in his face, cursed him in Arabic.

The other workers came over and laughed at him, and I got out of there and went home. Now my father came home irritated and yelled at me "How could you punch the manager? He is your boss!" I told him I was sick of this Ashkenazi garbage boss, who wouldn't teach me, this great friend of my father's. How my father loved Ashkenazim. To this day I cannot understand why; all of the Hebrew letters get stuck in their scrawny, ashen throats.

In any case I was happy that I always blocked up the toilets in the factory or scratched their polished furniture. No one knew and no one saw; there were always screams and yells of the managers: "Why don't you cover the furniture with blankets when you lift them into the trucks?" No one paid attention, and I would laugh and run away from the place. I always took revenge on people who upset me, but quietly.

After I quit working for the carpenter, my father, of course, wanted me to find something else; he came home and said he had another job for me in the circus. The Jerusalem municipality had brought elephants and lions to the city and erected a big tent in the city park for two weeks. I went there and the circus manager told me that I would be the *sadran*, organizing where things went, the equipment, the cages.

"Okay," I agreed. They gave me the job, and I had barely started when the manager came to me. He said "Leave this; come and watch the animals at night." I followed him, and he stood me in the center, surrounded by cages filled with various stinking animals, and they were scary, even though they were caged.

I was filled with fear. I left and went home. They sought me out and called the employment office and asked where I was. I told the manager to send his wife and kids to sit all night like that. If something happened, if an animal escaped or was stolen, what could I do anyway?

So, I was sent for new work: planting trees in the hills of Jerusalem. Many immigrants from Iraq had arrived in Israel. The government did not know what to do with them. They all lived in transit camps and in huts and tents in the Talpiot neighborhood of Jerusalem.

The city organized trucks to pick them up at eight in the morning. They were collected, twenty-four people in each truck. The trucks went to a specific place in the hills, and the new workers had to plant, mostly pine trees. I was one of the new workers along with some of my friends, who were so desperate for work that they were forced to take what was available. They paid us per tree.

The manager, an Ashkenazi, would circle around with a pipe in his mouth smoking nonstop. At the end of the day, he would count the trees and check if they were planted deeply enough. We divided up the mountain and made symbols with stones. There was wind and rain, and we had only three pails of water to drink that we brought from Jerusalem.

The work was hard; it was work for prisoners, and the pay was minimal. Whoever planted more trees got more money. I was not physically strong. I got pains in my back and chafed hands and blisters.

My friends said "What a father you have! This is what he could find you." For a sixteen-year-old to climb and descend hills all day was exhausting; it was for all of the workers.

I will never forget the many immigrants from Morocco who came to Israel in the 1950s. Most of them had many children and lived in transit camps. They needed a lot of patience and love, and a quick financial solution from the employment ministry my father directed.

But he, with his five clerks, would close himself in a room around a big table and gossip over tea and coffee, with heat in the winter and air conditioning in the summer, and barely answered these poor people, who came and stood in line and needed help to make money or a needed signature on a paper.

These poor, new immigrants became angry, cursed, screamed, and then the clerks would phone the police. My father took his frustrations out on my mother and then ate, lay down with a newspaper, and slept.

The party my father worked for and supported called itself the Workers' Party, but I assure you, they did not work too hard. At 3:00 p.m., he woke up from his nap (the office was open from 8:00 to noon), he had coffee, and, he went back to work from 4:00 to 6:00. Then he returned home for dinner.

My grandfather knew what my father was doing. I would meet him and kiss his hand and hug him; he was very clean and he often advised me to keep my body physically and spiritually pure. He never said a bad word about his son; he spoke to give me strength. He was thin with a hunchback, like his wife.

I will never forget: I once saw him when my father suggested work for him fixing the roads and sidewalks in Jerusalem for the municipality. My father took me to see my grandfather on Hillel Street and to ask the manager how his work was going. I went there and it broke my heart to see him, my dear grandfather, the *tzadik*, working with heavy tools and lifting stones.

And I can still see my father, sitting all day in his office on a chair and letting his own father work so hard. Naturally, my grandfather lasted a few days with difficulty and left. The manager told him it was not for him.

With happiness my parents divorced in the presence of the rabbinate. My father was home for the last time to take his things, as few as they were. He rented a place in the neighborhood of P. The main thing was he was far from us. He kept his job as the manager of the employment ministry. It was a good job with all of the benefits, and it occupied him.

Daily, he was in a bad mood; most of the time he argued with all of the employees. They worked behind a door of iron with a little window with bars on it, like a jail. He ate anything as long as it was cheap, and for lunches he went home to his mother to enjoy her soup and hilbeh.

He was entertained by his Labor Party meetings in the evenings at the new club on Jaffa. They gathered to kiss each other's behinds. Many people came to the club out of no choice; to get work and to get the pink slip, a square of pink paper that allowed them to collect unemployment benefits. Generally, the membership dues automatically came off the paychecks.

My littlest cousin lived with us like a brother. I barely saw him; he had been adopted by a complete stranger who took pity on him. My father was happy he did not have to make him a bar mitzvah. My middle brothers left for the kibbutz long ago.

My father later remarried a widow. He met her through a matchmaker. She had lost her husband in the Six Day War; we heard about this from people who like to gossip.

Mother immediately rented the extra room in the house to a girl from overseas after the divorce, and she continued to cook and clean for Ashkenazim in Rehavia when she felt strong enough. She often went to the shuk, the market, to shop and gather bones, meat and vegetables for the dog, Foxy, who still protected the house. He also guarded the colorful chickens and the big rooster who controlled them all day. The roses and spices grew wonderfully, and there was quiet and peace.

I could see that my mother finally felt free, but it was not a big change for her socially; she had already been without a husband, in the real sense, for years. She no longer liked men; she thought they were all like him.

She had some divorced and widowed Yemenite girlfriends who met with her at shul, and every man whose name came up was showered with endless curses. Their hands were lifted to the skies with a prayer to Hashem that He should pay them back.

My relatives were happy that finally this marriage was over. I did not forfeit my grandparents and saw them often, when my father was not around. For their part, they said Hashem does what He sees fit and were quiet.

Your mother tells me, Mirileh, that he asked for forgiveness from me and mother at my mother's funeral. What did this matter? He died one year after her and he is buried beside her. Can you imagine?

There must have been some kind of mix-up or confusion. My mother must have turned over in her grave at my father's burial. It took her two decades to get her divorce, and in the end, he lies beside her forever. The last time I went to the Mount of Olives to visit them, I stood beside my mother's grave and cried like a baby.

As you know, Miri, my mother died before her time and I did not merit to help her much after I moved to Canada. In those days Canada was much farther away than it is today with computers. My brothers made the decisions. I stood quietly; I did not know you cannot say kaddish without a minyan. I said kaddish and your uncles and cousin said amen.

One time, on my first return to Israel with your mother and your brother, in 1971, I went to visit my father. My middle brother convinced me that I must. I went with your mother to the Jerusalem neighborhood, B. H., and we entered the apartment.

I approached my father and kissed him and showed him your brother. He was two-years-old. My father, his grandfather, barely looked at him. His second wife sat beside him and tried to laugh, while he started to talk nonsense. I said "*Yalla*, I am going." I gave it to my brother on the head, and I said "It is a pity I listened to you." I don't listen to him anymore.

Even my mother never liked her middle sons. Some of us had to merit resembling my father. They were lucky living on the kibbutz; they did not endure the years of screaming and the divorce, as I did.

My father promised to take revenge on me for testifying against him at the divorce trial. And he did. One sunny day, on a Shabbat afternoon, in the heat of the day, we were coming home to sleep and rest. Mother went to her friends to tell them about the court's decision, and everyone was happy for her. Suddenly, I heard knocking at the door and yelling.

"Open up!" someone was screaming. The loud voice woke me up, and I opened the door, and saw a face of boiling anger.

I said "What gives?"

"This is my house, and you have no right to close the door." It was my father. There were still some of my father's belongings on the balcony, he threw them at me and said "I will still show you."

After half an hour the police arrived, and four policemen came out and asked me my name and the address of the house. I said they had the correct name and address. They handcuffed me and arrested me. I asked why, and they told me I should be embarrassed for hitting my father.

He had complained to the police. They threw me in the car, and I did not have a chance to speak. No one was home. The neighbors saw from the windows. My mother returned home and was informed by the neighbors that I had been taken away by the police. I am sure she was as shocked as I was.

I was put in a cell with four prisoners who looked at me and asked me what I had done to get myself arrested. I said nothing, and they laughed and said they had done nothing as well. I sat on a stinking mattress, angry, and irritated and worried what would happen to Mother. They gave us dinner, and I did not touch it. I did drink the coffee, and later I fell asleep on the filthy mattress.

In the morning, a policeman called V. took me out and I went to his office. He said my father's complaint was cancelled because the arresting officer requested a medical certificate and my father refused to provide one.

"He lied. Now take a lawyer and sue him for unlawful arrest."

I left the police station, which was in the Russian Compound, about a fifteen-minute walk from my home. I went straight home, and when my mother saw me, she treated me as though the Messiah had arrived.

She said, "Don't worry, God will punish him. He is so bad." I did not want to take him to court. I did not want to see him. I was embarrassed. All the neighbors came to shake my hand.

I thought for a few days about a new family name and told my brothers that from then on what my last name would be; if they wanted, they could change their last name too. I went to court and changed my last name. When it was my time to marry, I did not invite him and if he would have appeared, I would have thrown him out.

Mother began to have stomach pains. Her eyesight and hearing weakened. This all came from a life with no quiet and endless worries. What amazed me was how my parents managed to bring more children into this world. They were never together and hated each other; still every six years they had a boy they did not know what to do with. When my mother was sick in the nights, it was me who ran for the doctor. In the morning, my father would ask what happened, and I would tell him, but he was only interested in knowing if we had a receipt for the money so he could get a refund.

The screaming and fighting only worsened over the years, all about money. At the end of every month, my mother needed to ask for money and every Friday for money for Shabbat items, and so the storm would begin. He always wanted to know "Where is the money that I gave you last week? What did you do with it?"

The amount of money my father gave my mother was so little, maybe twenty liras, and, of course, not enough for me and three little brothers and later an adopted one. I was the big one, always caught in the middle. My father's parents, my grandparents the ones who lived without readily available water or electricity, down four flights of stairs in a basement, enjoyed only peace and happiness in their home. We had lights, running water, a huge garden, and nothing but misery.

Her sisters never believed my mother when she told them about her marriage. This caused her many tears. My father would visit them and charm them in Tel Aviv, and they were taken in by him. For my uncles, he got jobs driving mail trucks around and the like. Jobs like tree planting were reserved only for me, his eldest son, so no one believed us. He knew how to play the game.

Once my mother complained to my father's boss that he never gave her a dime, and my father screamed, and mother jumped two meters from the gazozstra —thankfully she did not break her leg. When my mother finally took D. a lawyer, we went to the Rabbinate for the first time. There were four rabbis as usual, three Ashkenazim and one Yemenite, Rabbi M. our neighbor.

Another terrible incident that happened with my father was after I returned from the Six Day War. He saw me on the streets of Jerusalem, downtown and said to my face, "*Haval sh'hazartah*, a pity you returned."

It is hard to believe, but it is true, a father telling his son it is a pity that he survived the war. It hurts me now to write this to you. When the war was over, I brought mother a lot of food in boxes and warm blankets as a present from the Egyptian army. She was happy to see me and blessed me and the gifts—especially the warm blankets.

In the end, my mother had a terrible death, falling from a cliff and ending up food for animals. It was months before her body was discovered. What did my mother do?

What crime? My father? He found a nice widow from the old days that did everything for him and lived in peace and quiet until the end. I know you are asking yourself, Miri, how my father's second marriage could be so different. I can only guess that he was worn out by then. I suppose even he got tired of fighting.

*

If I could I'd expand my father's letters, ghostwrite over his memories. I'd include his first wife, Emuna—the wife he has never brought up in fifty years.

"Emuna! Come. Let us get the blessing of the rabbi before we make our engagement official. "

"But why? I love you and you love me and that is enough."

"After my parents' marriage and divorce, you understand? I want blessings, as much as we can get."

"As you wish. We will go in the morning."

The insertion would be in vain. It is obvious these characters are made of wood. I imagine Emuna as a girl with unusually red hair. (I have never seen a photograph of her.) Her hair reaches to her shoulders, and it is her nicest feature.

It is not the storybook red of talking fire engines and smiling traffic lights, but a red somewhere between orange and brown, like freshly dug clay. She is slender and her skin has the glow of sunlight on water.

My father is strong and straight-backed from his year training to be a paratrooper in the army. He comes in uniform with his boots polished and his red beret is precisely angled. His new moustache is clipped; a black frown occupies his lips and his dark brown eyes are apprehensive. He looks more like a soldier on guard duty after an alarm has gone off than a would-be groom with his bride.

My father had no vision for him and his would-be wife. All he did have was a tremendous desire for change; like a man who has been carrying a bulging sack of coal over his shoulder for so long, he cannot tell if his hands are black because the sun set long ago, or if his eyes are closed.

White Zion

The telephone rings, but this time I do not answer. On Friday afternoon it can only be one person: my father calling long distance from Ottawa. I sense cold northern winds rifling through the papers on my desk in Israel.

As though in anticipation, ice crystals are forming on the edges of my windowsill and I shiver. But they are only my daughters' latest offerings from *gan*: beaded hairbands in Shabbat-white. The phone remains in its cradle, but my father's unspoken words penetrate; salt pellets eroding black ice. Words half-frozen with backed-up emotion "I've lost my *kaddish*," he says in guttural Hebrew, over and over with hardly a break, like hailstones falling on glass.

In British-Occupied Jerusalem there were quandaries as deep and impenetrable as snowbanks in winter's old age. He has forgotten that he overcame them. But I know it is not so simple; it is the thought of the next world that drums in his ears; making it harder for him to pump iron, jog, argue. In his youth, death was only for those who couldn't dodge the bombs and bullets quickly enough and he was quick, now death is a stop on a train he cannot disembark.

"My father didn't live too long and my poor mother, who knows what she did to deserve her death? She was food for animals, *Hashem yishmor*. I know my grandfather and grandmother are waiting for me in *shamayim* and when they ask me, *Hakadosh Baruch hu*, what will I answer?"

The baby stirred and I had to go. He acknowledged my rushed apology, and another layer of frost formed between us; he has to return to his self-imposed silence the moment he hangs up.

My father's paternal grandparents, Yaakov and Sara, lived a ten-minute walk away from the neighborhood where he grew up, where his younger brothers will no longer set foot. It was a predominantly Yemenite neighborhood in Jerusalem in 1936: pitiable, deprived, disfavored. They lived on J. Street, an extension of *Mahane Yehudah*, a busy outdoor fresh food market.

"They were *tzadikim*, holy people. They came to Palestine because the *Rav* said it's time to go to Zion and meet the *Moshiach*. My grandfather carried my father, three-months-old, on his back from Aden. If you know Aden you know there was nothing there, and it was hot like *azazel*. The ground is narrow, not easy, lots of rocks, no real roads and the ship was packed, you couldn't move. They came to *Mitsrayim*, an Egyptian port and what were the people after so long time on the water? No food, sick to death half of them, *ganavim* everywhere if you weren't watching your one or two things. Also, my mother's family, your great grandparents, came same time, same way."

I knew by the hollow sound in his voice that my father regretted the distance between him and his maternal grandparents. They got off at the first stop: Jaffa, settling in the sand dune nearby that was Tel Aviv.

In Palestine travel between Jerusalem and Tel Aviv was difficult and costly, so he rarely saw them. He was close to his father's parents, Yaakov and Sara, even after his own parents divorced.

Having come all the way to the home of the Messiah, the young Yemenite couple wanted to live on his doorstep, so they continued the eighty-seven kilometers by train to Jerusalem. The poorly paved streets were broken and Jerusalemites lived behind towering iron gates, which remained open only as long as it was daylight. At night people were afraid to sleep unless the gates were locked. In a land of Turkish rulers and obeyers, Sara had four sons and no daughters.

In the basement they called home the only light was that of the Torah for Yaakov spent every spare moment bent over the Talmud. The windowless enclave lacked electricity and running water was unheard of. He was a contented man, devoted to his religious duties, his wife, and his sons. When he was not studying, he was a *shochet*, a ritual slaughterer mostly of chickens and he was the *gabai*, the sexton, of the Yemenite synagogue upstairs.

My father would inhale deeply as he spoke of his grandmother's cooking, the fresh *saluf*, Yemenite pitas, she sold to passers-by. He told me proudly that she took up the mantel of the *mikvah* lady at sunset, inspecting Jewish women according to the Law, before they dipped in the ritual bath. In this atmosphere of deference to God's will, my grandfather, Mordechai, was raised. But you do not have to hear more than one of my father's stories to know that as a married man he chose a different path.

When I was old enough to notice I asked my father why he was so much older than his brothers.

"The screaming in my house was nonstop," he began between mouthfuls of green salad, topped with oily humus and red *schug*. "After me they told my mother, don't have more children. The pregnancy hurt her hearing, her eyes, made her almost blind *b'emet*. Her whole body was no good after, weak. How she and my father every six years came with a son, I don't know. Every six years a son for twenty-five years."

With that he shook his head, his powerful neck turning on his wide back, his face reflecting his bewilderment; an overgrown child lost in the swirl of a storm. I never saw my paternal grandfather and my father seemed to be glad of it; a revenge so weak it wouldn't melt the snow in your gloves.

"He made me go to that Ashkenazi school and I hated it, you wouldn't believe. I was the only one dark in the class, only me. And the teacher? German, Jewish, Ashkenazi mamzer, he would twist my ear until I cried. For nothing and it hurt all right and he would laugh. My father, he was not interested. He worked for *Mapai*, the left-wing government and he sat all day in air conditioning in the summer; in the winter he had heat and that's all into it, *naal abuk*. What kind of father? *Drek*! Him and the Ashkenazim together. Don't worry. I got him back that teacher. I waited ten years, can you believe? Quietly for my chance. Then when I was in the army before I was paratrooper—you listening, Miri?"

"Sure Abba, I'm listening, *bevadai*."

I could not risk telling him that I knew this story the way other children know Cinderella or Snow White, that I'd only wanted to know about the age difference between him and his siblings.

He might mutter *beseder*, okay, and shrug his bare shoulders—he rarely wore shirts indoors, even in deep winter—or he might get angry, insulted, and then you never knew what would happen. Sometimes he shouted about a lack of respect, other times his look became so menacing, it seemed best to go upstairs for a while, freeze behind a closed door until bedtime.

My father was denied tales of wicked stepmothers, sly wolves hiding behind thick trees and pretty, blond fairy godmothers. He put my brother, Our-Stan, and me to sleep with tales of Ashkenazi teachers, who taunted a helpless boy who stood out, Yemenite fathers who locked a sweet son outside to sleep with the chickens and goats until the sun rose.

There was an evil German kindergarten teacher, Anni, who forced her three-year-old charges to eat their own vomit. She doubled as a boarder, renting the spare room in a little boy's home with her husband and two young daughters. With her bare hands, she drowned the mice that infested the house in a deep ceramic bowl.

Like all fairytales there were satisfying endings; the teachers always got their comeuppance when their Vespas crashed into cliffs, separating into hundreds of useless pieces and settling in the valley below at the end of Jerusalem, having been tossed over the edge of a mountain by the champion, my father and his powerful biceps.

Sometimes the ending was a good-for-nothing father begging for forgiveness to his first-born son's wife and receiving only silence. Another favorite conclusion was a German Jewish teacher, passed out on his desk, having ingested the sleeping pills the heroic boy stole from his sick mother and crushed into the government-sponsored portion of daily milk, distributed in all state-run Israeli schools.

Sometimes my father repeated his stories or parts of them over breakfast if he suspected we had drifted into sleep and missed the finale. "No one is going to screw me. Don't trust nobody. All of them, Hashem should burn them up."

Then he would rise and open the cupboard, seeking one of his favorite low sugar cereals, maybe Shredded Wheat or Grape Nuts. He filled the skim milk to the rim of the oversized bowl. As a child I gaped at my father while he ate, like he was the largest fish in an aquarium, the one people point to and wonder about; does it eat the other fish?

"I used to walk to school three kilometers all the way to the end of Jaffa Road," my father said softly, as he smoothed my eyebrows over and over with his strong, warm hands and wrapped my blanket tighter around my body. Our-Stan was listening from his bed across the room, waiting for his turn.

My father smelled like Irish Spring soap and Vaseline Intensive Care hand lotion. With all of his weight lifting, and dishwashing, there were no rough edges to my father's hands and they were impervious to the below-zero temperatures. His touch was as smooth as new snow and not just regular warm; each finger seemed to radiate a therapeutic heat. I never had a head or neckache that did not evaporate under my father's hands, like the enemies in the stories he loves to tell.

"What if it rained?"

"Rain, shmain. You worry about rain because you are soft, Canadian. A little bit of cold and you are crying already. I worry about the *p'satsot*. They were bombing us those Arabs, all the time, every second, no stop. Across from our house was the *beit avot*, cemetery, and all night crying, screaming of the families over the dead. The dead were piled so high, there were not enough people to bury them and the crying you wouldn't believe, all night long. I could hear them. *Oy Elohim.*

Those bombs. We used to hear the sound of them coming and right away, we ran to the bathtub. That's what they told us, the safest place. But my mother she was brave, she sat and watched them fall. "

Our-Stan always sat up at the mention of bombs, jeeps, tanks, anything that was connected with weapons and war. But I was not fascinated, only scared. To me it was a tale of an unreal place, my father himself became unreal at those times.

I remember reaching out at points in the story to touch his forearms or the backs of his hands, just to see. I longed to connect the storyteller to the person who looked and sounded like my father, the one who rose at 5 a.m. each morning to lift weights in the unfinished basement before he began defrosting the station wagon—we never owned a garage.

It took thirty minutes every morning to sweep the foot of snow that had fallen on the roof of the car during the night, to chip the ice off the side mirrors, or at least defrost a circle large enough to make driving possible, to coax life back into the windshield wipers that lay frozen in whatever position they had been in when the key was removed from the ignition.

"Today the Knesset is right across the street and the courthouse, but then? Nothing. Fields. Fields and Arab villages empty, gone. One morning we woke up and they had all run away and that is when the war started. I wanted to go to the school close to the house, with my friends, with the other Yemenite, but no my father said and he never listened to nobody. Three kilometers I had to walk, both ways and listen for bombs. What was there to do? We did what he told us. If not, he shouted to wake the dead and he wouldn't give us, not a lira. The mortgage he'd say. But he was a *shakran*. The mortgage he paid long before."

The smell filling my home reminded me to check the oven: the *challahs* were almost ready. My baby is unable to digest the white sesame seeds, the common topping for egg-bread in Israel. I know poppy seeds are not the same plant but fear her reaction all the same; an ugly, red, raised rash that spreads from under her hairline at the back of her neck to her tailbone. Instead, I smear raw egg on the soft dough, they'd look glazed; that would make them stand out from the weekday bread.

On the wall leading out of the kitchen the framed black and white photograph of my father as a paratrooper in the Sinai War hangs. His beret and satisfied smile show off his good looks. Next to him are Sara and Yaakov, newly arrived in the Ottoman Empire; the latter's long *peyot* are neat and curled and he is in traditional robe-like dress, only Sara's face is visible, as she is covered Arab-style in white, including her girlish throat. My father's mother is on the end; she is modestly posing as the new Miss Tel Aviv in British-Occupied Palestine.

In my kitchen the natural light is fading. I turn off the oven but leave the challahs inside. There will be warm fresh bread with our meal. I check the clock on the stove for the last time, call the girls over. Together we light Shabbat candles. Then we cover our eyes with our hands to make the blessing. Between their fingers, my daughters peek, but I pretend not to notice. We look out the large windows onto the Yarkon Park, as we do every Friday at sundown.

Where my father sits there are still seven hours until candle-lighting. My brother has announced his choice of bride; from the rearview mirror of her SUV a white, crystal rosary dangles, and catches the glare of the snowdrifts, piled high on either side of the Queensway.

Modest Things

"I was at the bus stop after the game and it was getting dark. A man came up to me. He looked like a chassid," Ruby said. Then he paused. I admit I was paying scant attention to the rabbi's son, my own son's guest for Shabbat lunch.

But something in Ruby's voice made me stop picking up the scattered building blocks and marbles. I turned to look at the nine-year-old in his white button-down shirt and black pants, both already grass stained from a pre-breakfast soccer game with his two brothers and my son, Elazar.

"Are you speaking to me, sweetie?" I asked Ruby. It was rare that Elazar's friends addressed me unless they were confused about the location of the bathroom or were desperate for a glass of water. Ruby nodded. "Go on then," I continued.

The boy shifted on my black, leather couch. He was tall for his age and might have passed for eleven. I had heard other parents ask him if he was preparing for his bar mitzvah, but his voice lacked the pitch of a boy starting to turn into a man.

It occurred to me then that he had eaten nothing, but a few bites of chicken breast at lunch. We listened to the ticking of the clock for another minute. Finally, Ruby took a deep breath and spread his palms flat on his knees.

"You know, I finish school around four o'clock," he said.

I nodded and passed the boy a plate of chocolate cupcakes covered in bubblegum-pink sprinkles and miniature white marshmallows. He shook his head.

"Stop doing stuff and sit down, Mom. Ruby wants to tell you something," Elazar pleaded.

"Okay. I only thought he might like a Shabbat treat."
"Mom!"
"I'm listening. Go ahead, Ruby," I said.
I sat in the rocking chair facing Ruby.

"So, I get out at four o'clock, but the bus only comes an hour later. I went to play basketball with some other boys," Ruby said. He stopped talking again and his eyes shifted from my own to Elazar's. My son nodded at his friend and raised his hands slowly toward him as if to draw the words out of Ruby's mouth. I thought of heat drawing pain from muscle.

"Why are you stopping again?" Elazar asked.

"No, I'm not stopping. I'm just trying to find the words in English," Ruby answered. "The man wore black pants and a black hat. He had a beard." Ruby passed his hand over his chin as if to show me a long beard. "He asked me if I wanted to do him a favor. He said please."

Then Ruby's eyes met mine. It took me a minute to understand: He wanted my nod to tell him that it was perfectly all right to speak to a stranger who looked religious.

"Yes, a religious man came up to you. Go on," I said. Ruby's facial muscles relaxed.

I thought then about how many times each day we told our children how critical it was to help those in need, how much blessing it brought into the world.

Elazar's hand was suddenly shaking my shoulder. "Mommy, can I have another cupcake?"

I glanced at him. "Yes, you may," then returned my attention to Ruby. "Go on."

"I went with the chassid and he walked back into the Old City. You know, my bus stop is outside the walls. We went down paths, turned here, turned again." Ruby motioned with both hands as he spoke. His fingers were closed together, so they looked like two snakes crossing paths. "We came to a room. It was like a cave. Then he—" Ruby stopped again and a shadow darkened his face. He looked at the tiled floor. "I don't know how to say it in English," he mumbled.

"Say it in Hebrew. It's okay," I said.

"He took out his immodest thing," Ruby blurted.

I jumped in my chair, as though a liter of milk had crashed to the floor, and Elazar looked at me, his eyebrows knitted together.

"What's that?" he whispered, with one hand cupped around the side of his mouth.

"I'll tell you later. Shush," I answered.

Ruby did not raise his eyes.

"What did he do, sweetie?" I asked.

"He took my hand and I had no idea what was in my hand. I could not see. Then I knew—I don't know how I knew—and I turned and ran. I ran away."

"What is he saying, Mommy? What did the chassid do? What is an immodest thing?" Elazar asked.

"I wanted to tell you, Mrs. Ehrblich," Ruby whispered. Tears darkened his green eyes and now they were the color of grass stains.

"It's good that you told me."

I sighed at the childishly decorated cupcakes on the table, and the tiny marshmallows suddenly appeared as though they would fall off with the slightest touch. They were so fragile; I should have used chocolate chips. Such silly thoughts to be going through my head then.

"Ruby?"

"Yes, Mrs. Ehrblich?"

I stopped talking because when I looked up, I saw Ruby running through the Old City streets, beads of sweat at his temples, his hand held out in front of him. He was racing by rabbis in knee-length black coats, Catholic priests in black, nuns in black, Muslims on their way to prayers, tourists with cameras that doubled as cellular phones, who had just placed prayer notes in the cracks of the Wailing Wall. He was trying to find his way back to the bus stop, but he was unsure. Had they turned left or right on C. Street? Where was his school?

"When someone tells you they need a favor, someone big, you tell them to please ask an adult."

"Yes, Mrs. Ehrblich."

"Mommy! What happened?" Elazar asked.

"I'll tell you soon."

My son was halfway through his second cupcake. The remains of the first one showed on his white shirt, marshmallow stuck to his cheek; at the bathroom sink, Ruby was washing his hands, again and again.

I Put Him on the Bottle

"It was so interesting," my mother began. "I was watching a program on children sleeping in their parents' beds. They were saying that for many people it goes on way too long."

"Really?" I responded, not at all interested.

I was exhausted from my hour-long bus ride home from school and my stomach was still bothering me from a bug I had had over the weekend. But I could see my mother was starving for some adult conversation after a full day of looking after my children of two, four and six, so I'd have to wait before taking the shower I'd been envisioning since lunch time.

"They interviewed a man who had divorced his first wife because she wouldn't take the kids out of the bed and here he was married again with the same problem. Imagine?"

"Hmm," I answered, struggling with my eyelids.
I realized that I had to say something or risk appearing rude.

"Well, you know the Torah would say that marital harmony comes first. Even if the mother wants the child in the bed, if the father is insistent and it's damaging the marriage, the father's wishes take precedence."

My mother's frown was unexpected.

"The father's wishes come first, do they?"

"Well, yes." My eyes were open now. "Unless he is asking his wife to commit a sin. Take nursing for example."

I paused to take a sip of water and couldn't help but notice that my mother was suddenly sitting up, erect and alert.

"If the husband wants his wife to stop nursing because he feels that his wife is not getting pregnant and he wants another child, this is forbidden. That is considered stealing his baby's rightful milk to give to another child. If mother and baby are happy nursing, she has every right to refuse."

"Really? For nursing?"

"Yes."

I put my head down on the couch again and closed my eyes, but felt my mother was still sitting up obviously wanting me to continue. I was too tired to indulge her. I had nursed all of my children to a month short of two years and she had been supportive, even though I knew that she had never nursed any of us. She had always told me that it had been unfashionable in her day. It had been considered unhygienic and unreliable.

In my half-sleep, guilt began to cover me like a down comforter in July. She had flown all the way from Canada so that I could attend a summer writing workshop and not feel guilty about leaving my children with a stranger.

"Maybe you can help me with my homework?" I offered.

"What homework?"

Her voice had soured. I had changed the subject.

"Well, my professor—"

"Oh, your professor— Where's he from?"

"He's from Boston. You know, no *r*'s and long *a*'s"

"Boston? Oh yes, that accent. Like the Kennedys."

"Yes, Mom, just like the Kennedys."

"Okay, go on."

"He gave us some ideas for a short story, and one of them was to write the story you would never tell."

"Oh."

"So?"

My mother rubbed her hands together, but her mouth remained closed.

"Well, you have lots of stories," I said finally.

"Why are you asking me? Don't you have any?"

"He's into secrets, family secrets. Besides you're older."

As calm and gentle as she appeared to be, I knew my mother had lots of riveting stories. She had an ex-husband, a high school sweetheart, she had been famous as a child actress, a two-time winner of the best actress in Canada award and, of course, there was her Sophia Loren-like beauty.

Beautiful women have their own stories: prominent judges seeking mistresses, other people's husbands calling them at peculiar hours.

"Don't think that old stereotype doesn't ring true," I remember my mother telling me when I first married. "You know the one about divorced women? 'You must be lonely in the night,'" she began, instantly adopting a male voice. "'I could comfort you.' Imagine! To this day some of my best friends don't know how their husbands phoned me. And we used to go out with these couples every Saturday night!"

I had been living in Israel for so long that I had forgotten.

"Secrets. Oh dear. Does he want us to get personal?"

My mother said the word *personal* in a low voice, like somebody else might say cancer or Down syndrome. In spite of her childhood career, she was a conservative soul by nature and nurture, no swearing, no raised voices and she'd start giggling if any alcohol appeared within arm's reach.

"Goodness, wine," she'd say and hastily add, "Jews don't drink, dear," as though I were in any danger of overdosing on the thick sticky-sweet, cough-syrupy wine my Zaide used for *kiddush* on Friday nights.

"Well, it is supposed to be a story you wouldn't want to tell anyone."

There was silence. My eyes closed again. Sleep tapped me on the shoulder insistently and I turned toward it.

"Do you want to know why I couldn't nurse your brother, Jonathan?"

My eyes responded, but only underneath closed lids. Jonathan was the oldest of the eight of us. Was it not unfashionable and unhygienic? Was this not part of the family inheritance the professor had spoken about? I must have been told that story dozens of times while I nursed my own babies.

"It was a terrible labor; nineteen hours and he was breach. Well, you know all of that." I nodded. "I was only twenty, inexperienced, completely naive. What did we know in the fifties? I wanted to nurse Jonathan. Nobody was doing it then, but I wanted to. But his father, he wanted to... to nurse on me instead!"

My mother paused, but I had not digested her words.

"He kept insisting, 'You look so beautiful, it's so beautiful. That milk is for me. Let me nurse on you.'"

"He wanted his baby's milk?" I stammered.

"He didn't just want it, he insisted on it. He begged me for it. He kept saying, 'My mother never nursed me. This beautiful warm milk coming from you, it's mine.' He wrestled me for it. From our son, crying with hunger. Our week-old son."

My mother's eyes clouded and I could feel the storm in her slim body. I couldn't find words, but she didn't seem to expect any.

"I had no one to talk to, to tell. I have no sisters, and your Bubby? Imagine! She would have been hysterical. How could I tell my friends? I had no experience with men. Maybe that's how they all were? Who knew? I can still see him on his knees beseeching me, pleading. He was too aggressive for me. A tax lawyer, a good family, huh! To this day, I see his father in *shul* every Shabbat. He's 101, can you believe that?"

"What did you do?" I asked slowly, trying to imagine myself in her place.

"I would say, 'Are you crazy or what? This is Jonathan's milk!' But I was defenseless. If he would even see my breasts leaking, you know when they get engorged, you fill up, if he would even notice it, he would start. 'That's my milk. Oh, please nurse me. It's so beautiful, so beautiful.'"

I could see my mother's burning humiliation, her quiet resentment. Jonathan is forty-eight today, but at that moment he was an innocent baby. His own father was robbing him; his mother was powerless, infantilized like him.

"I was so stupid," she repeated. "What did I know? What did I know about men?"

The woman before me was suddenly twenty; the sixty-eight-year-old *savta*, who had served noodles only an hour ago, singing "Twinkle Little Star," absent. Her bewilderment and shame were as fresh as a newborn's, and her cry just as powerful.

"Finally, at four months I just stopped. I couldn't take it anymore. I put him on a bottle. My beautiful baby boy. I felt so guilty, but what choice did I have? I never even tried nursing the other three. They gave me pills in the hospital. I couldn't go through that again. That probably sounds pitiful to you, but it wasn't done in my day—divorce. But I finally did it. I finally left him and his craziness behind. Did you know Canada used to have a clause in separation agreements called the chastity belt clause? A woman was supposed to sign that if she were ever seen with another man, her husband could take her children away from her. But he could do whatever he wanted! I refused to sign it. I finally forced him out of the house and within a year I met your father. For six years now, I've been watching you nurse your babies. Don't you ever wonder how I've looked at you sometimes?"

"No," I whispered. "I never..."

"Well, you nurse your babies my baby. Don't let anyone tell you anything else."

I knew she was referring to my mother-in-law, who considered nursing on par with munching sweet hay, chewing the cud, and other favorite pastimes of cows. I had often complained to my own mother about this. She was always encouraging, but how could I have known?

ABOUT THE AUTHOR

Canadian Gila Green is a writer, editor, and EFL teacher.
As the daughter of a Yemenite-Israeli father and an
Ashkenazi-Canadian mother, she often writes about the
immigrant experience, including dislocation, alienation, and
racism. She spent time in South Africa before settling in Israel
where she lives with her husband and five children.

She is the author of *White Zion* and two adult novels: *Passport
Control* and *King of the Class* and her short works have appeared
in dozens of literary magazines and anthologies. Her new
young adult novel *No Entry* is forthcoming in 2019 and is the
first in an environmental series.
Please visit Gila www.gilagreenwrites.com

www.ingramcontent.com/pod-product-compliance
Lightning Source LLC
Chambersburg PA
CBHW030342030726
47499CB00003B/874